A   N

illustrated by Meryl Henderson

ANDREW JACKSON

Young Patriot

by George Edward Stanley

ALADDIN PAPERBACKS

New York   London   Toronto   Sydney   Singapore

This book is a work of fiction. Any references to historical events,
real people, or real locales are used fictitiously. Other names,
characters, places, and incidents are the product of the author's imagination,
and any resemblance to actual events or locales or persons,
living or dead, is entirely coincidental.

First Aladdin Paperbacks edition May 2003

Text copyright © 2003 by George Edward Stanley
Illustrations copyright © 2003 by Meryl Henderson

ALADDIN PAPERBACKS
An imprint of Simon & Schuster Children's Publishing Division
1230 Avenue of the Americas
New York, NY 10020

Designed by Lisa Vega
The text of this book was set in Adobe Garamond.
Printed in the United States of America

2   4   6   8   10   9   7   5   3   1

Library of Congress Control Number 2002107421
ISBN 0-689-85744-6

ILLUSTRATIONS

PAGE

Andy read out loud the stories on the front page.   4

A thick cloud of red dust almost hid the cattle and the
drovers.   17

Mr. Lowe was standing on his porch, a musket in his hands.   38

From the interior of the fort, they would heave the cannonballs
toward the British fleet.   57

Charles Town was even more beautiful than Jimmy had
promised.   81

What Andy witnessed that afternoon would stay with him
for the rest of his life.   92

As Andy darted out the door bullets whizzed above his head.   130

Suddenly the officer withdrew his sword and swung it hard
at Andy.   137

Just before his mother disappeared from sight, she turned
once more and waved to him.   174

Andy went to every cockfight in the city.   209

They packed their belongings and joined the wagon train.   237

He started raising thoroughbred horses.   245

CONTENTS

PAGE

Why Do I Have to Go to
School?   1

The Jacksons Come to
America   14

Wagon Train to Boston!   32

The Declaration of
Independence   50

The Cattle Drive to
Charles Town   63

War Comes to the
Waxhaws   86

Captured by the British! 108

PAGE

Prisoners of War   134

All Alone   161

Everyone Is Worried
about Andy   179

Andy Squanders His
Inheritance   193

Frontier Lawyer   216

Andrew and Rachel   241

Fighting the British—
Again!   247

President of the United
States   253

ANDREW JACKSON

Young Patriot

Why Do I Have to Go to School?

"Ouch!" eight-year-old Andrew Jackson cried. "You stuck me!"

"Well, if you don't stand still," his mother admonished him, "your leg is going to have more needle holes in it than your pants!"

"Why do I have to go to school anyway, Mother?" Andy said. "I already know more than the master does."

"Andy Jackson! You hush that kind of talk," his mother scolded. "I'll not hear any more of it."

Andy's cousin, Jemima Crawford, looked up from washing the dishes. "Andy's telling the truth, Aunt Betty," she said. "He's read all three of the books, and he knows how to do addition and subtraction better than the schoolmaster."

"Andy's teaching me how to add and subtract, Aunt Betty," Louisa, another one of his cousins, said. "I asked the schoolmaster to help me, but he said he was too sleepy."

Andy's mother let out a sigh, but she didn't say anything. Andy knew what she was thinking, though. He had overheard her talking to Aunt Jane, his mother's invalid sister.

"It's no school at all, Jane," she had said. "The people of South Carolina don't want to waste their money on a real school."

Andy knew his mother was right, although he'd never tell her so, because that would mean she'd probably want to send him somewhere else. Many times she had told him that her dream was for him to become a Presbyterian minister.

There are other things I want to do instead, Andy thought. He longed to see the rest of this new country. Over and over he listened to the stories that passing travelers would tell about what lay to the south and north of where the Crawfords and the Jacksons lived in the Waxhaws, that broad strip of land between Charlotte, North Carolina, and Lancaster, South Carolina.

The log cabin school that Andrew Jackson attended in that year of 1775 stood in a grove of scrub pine trees. The cabin was small, about twenty square feet, and its one door was hung by leather hinges. It had no windows.

Suddenly Andy had an idea. "Jemima!" he said. "Bring me that . . . ouch! . . . newspaper!"

Jemima dried her hands and picked up the copy of the Charles Town *Post*. It had been left yesterday by a traveler. She handed it to her cousin.

While his mother continued mending the tear in his pants, Andy read out loud the stories on the front page. They were mostly about events happening in far-off places, such as the battles at Lexington and Concord in Massachusetts and the meetings of the Second Continental Congress in Pennsylvania.

All of a sudden Andy forgot the reason he had wanted to read the newspaper to his mother in the first place—to prove to her that he didn't really need to go to school. Now all that he could think

about was how angry he was with the British, those people from across the wide Atlantic Ocean who thought they had the right to tell the Americans how to live their lives. One of these days, Andy vowed, he was going to fight these British!

"There!" Mrs. Jackson said. She cut the thread with a kitchen knife, tested the mend, and stood up. She ruffled Andy's red hair. "You need to take a brush to that before you go to school," she said. Without waiting for him to comment, she looked into his blue eyes and added, "I know you'd rather go with your uncle James on the cattle drive to Charles Town, Andy, instead of going to school, but then that's probably what you'd end up doing for the rest of your life."

"That wouldn't be so bad, Mother," Andy said. "I like taking care of the cattle. I like being outdoors. That school building is so hot and stuffy."

"Oh, Andy! You have so much potential," his mother said. She put her hands on his shoulders and drew him close to her. "I'm not against your helping your uncle James with the cattle, before and after school, because it's important that you do your share of the hard work around here, but the only way to get ahead in life is to get an education. Without an education, you'd be working in the fields from before the sun comes up until after it's gone down, with little to show for it except baked skin and callouses on your hands." She sighed deeply. "With your father dead, you and your brothers will have to make your own way. Learning is easy for you, Andy. It's not for Hugh and Robbie. That's why I insist that *you* go to school!"

School! Andy thought. He didn't even like the sound of that word.

Mrs. Jackson looked around the kitchen. "Chores done?" she said to her nieces.

Jemima and Louisa nodded.

"Then finish getting ready for school and go say good-bye to your mother," Mrs. Jackson said.

When Andy's father died, Mrs. Jackson's sister, Jane, had asked her and her three boys to come live with the Crawfords in the Waxhaws. Mrs. Crawford was an invalid and needed someone to help her with the household and to take care of her children. Mrs. Jackson, with no means of support for her and her three sons, accepted. It was a wonderful arrangement, for the combined families lived together in harmony. Mr. Crawford had promised Andy's mother that he would looked after her three sons as though they were his own, and he had kept that promise.

"I'll be outside with Uncle James," Andy shouted as he headed out the door.

"Stay off that rail fence," his mother shouted back to him. "I don't have time to mend your pants again!"

Andy knew he only had a few minutes before his brothers and his cousins would be ready to leave for school. He hurried outside once more to be around his uncle James and the other men, including his older Crawford cousins, Edward, George, and James Jr., whom everyone called Jimmy, as they thinned the herd for the drive south to Charles Town.

Andy wished he could be like some of South Carolina's wealthy settlers who raised cattle. He had heard his uncle James talking about how, when the first settlers arrived on the coast of South Carolina, they didn't find the vast forests that other settlers had found farther north along the coast. Instead, they found large areas of grassland and only patches of forest. They soon discovered why. The Indians that were native to the coastal areas regularly burned off the forests so that they could farm and hunt, and so they could also see their enemies approaching.

Although the early settlers of South Carolina brought with them only a few head of cattle, their cattle grew very fast on the rich and nourishing grass that was available. It didn't take a lot of effort to raise cattle—all the settlers had to do was to keep an eye on them as they ate their way through the available grass—so it wasn't long until they had huge herds. In order to keep their cattle in food, these settlers drove their large herds a hundred to two hundred miles to grasslands on coastal plains. When the herds were ready for market, the settlers would then drive their cattle to Charles Town or even to Philadelphia, in far-off Pennsylvania.

When Andy reached the cattle pen, he climbed up on the rail fence, this time being extra careful so that he wouldn't tear his pants again.

He knew he was disobeying his mother, but he wanted to sit beside his cousins as they told their hired hands which cows were to be taken out of the stock for the drive. Andy pretended he was the one yelling, "That brown one! This black one!" He knew he had a good eye for which cows would bring the most money at market.

"Andrew! Get down off the fence." Andy turned and saw his uncle James coming toward him. "I know for a fact that your mother told you not to climb back on there." When his uncle saw the incredulous look on Andy's face, he had to laugh. "I'm not a mind reader, son," he admitted. "I was getting a drink of water from the rain barrel just outside the kitchen window, and I heard what your mother said."

Andy grinned and climbed down.

"Let me go with you on the drive to Charles Town, Uncle James," Andy pleaded. "Mother doesn't understand. I'm bored in school. I already know everything."

His uncle James snorted. "No man should ever think that he knows everything, Andy," he said. "A really smart man is the first to admit that he knows very little."

"Well, what I meant is that, well, I know as much as . . . ," Andy tried to say.

But his uncle James held up a hand to silence him. "You know how important it is to your mother that you get a good education. It's important to me too," he said. "I've promised her that when you're old enough, I'll take you with me on one of the drives, but I need people who are really smart working for me, and you have to go to school to get smart. Andy, I think you've got a good head for knowing which cows to sell and which ones to fatten up some more—"

"I do, Uncle James!" Andy said, interrupting him. "I do!"

". . . but it's a long way to Charles Town, at least one hundred and sixty miles, and Charles Town is a big place, not like around here," his uncle continued. "If you get tired, I don't have time to carry you, and when we get to town, I don't have time to make sure you don't get into trouble."

Andy felt his temper rising, the temper he was famous for in school, the one that often got him in trouble for arguing with the schoolmaster and for fighting with some of the other boys in the class. It really made him angry when people thought he was a baby, that he couldn't take care of himself. Besides, if he was good enough to work for his uncle here on their farm, before school and after, then why wasn't he good enough to go with him on the drive to Charles Town?

But before Andy could say anything else, several of the steers closest to the fence where he was standing decided they weren't going to cooperate with the men trying to separate them from the herd. Most of the dust they stirred up landed on Andy.

Andy let loose with some colorful language. Now there was so much dirt in his eyes that he couldn't see and so much dirt in his mouth that that was all he could taste.

"Come on, Andy!" his cousins called to him. "We have to leave for school."

"Hold your horses!" he called to them.

It was useless, Andy knew, to keep talking to his uncle and his mother about not going to school and going on the cattle drive instead. They had made up their minds. When it came right down to it, he couldn't disobey them, even if in his heart he wanted to.

Andy hurried to the water pump and pumped out just enough water to smear most of the dust that had settled on him. Now he was even more miserable.

"Andy?"

Andy looked up to see his mother coming toward him.

"Yes, ma'am?" he said.

"When you were reading the Charles Town newspaper just a while ago, I was so proud of you," his mother said softly.

Andy shrugged. "It's nothing to be able to read, Mother," he said.

"Oh, but it is, Andy!" Mrs. Jackson said. "And your father would have been proud of you too!"

Andy felt a swelling in his throat. It always happened when his mother talked about his father. He guessed it had something to do with how much he missed having a father, although he tried hard not to think about it very much. After all, he had Uncle James.

"Tonight, after supper, I'm going to tell you all about your father and your grandfather and how we came to be in the Waxhaws," Mrs. Jackson said. She gave him a big smile.

"There are some things that I think you should know, now that you're getting older."

Hearing that, Andrew grinned. Had his mother really said that he was getting older? It was almost as good as going on the cattle drive with Uncle James.

"Now, off to school!" Mrs. Jackson said. "You're going to be late."

Andrew ran to catch up with his cousins, shouting "Wait for me!" as he did. Knowing now what awaited him that night, he was sure he could probably make it through one more day of school.

The Jacksons Come to America

Two hours later Andy was leaning his head on his school desk, which was really just a long wooden slab fastened to one wall, used by all of the students and made as smooth as possible by an ax. Andy was doing his best to stay awake as the schoolmaster read one of the longest and most boring poems that he had ever heard.

Why did his seat feel even harder today? Andy wondered. He shifted uncomfortably on the bark-free log and thought about building a chair like the one his mother sat in at home. Of course, that would probably make everyone think he planned to stay in school longer than he did.

All of a sudden, above the droning of the school-master's voice, Andy's ears picked up another sound he was very familiar with: the lowing of cattle. "Here it comes!" he shouted, interrupting the schoolmaster's recitation. "Here comes the cattle drive!"

When he had first got to school that morning, Andy asked the master if they could stop class and watch when the cattle drive came by. The school-master feigned disinterest in such an unscholarly activity but agreed that perhaps some in the class might find it interesting, from a purely intellectual standpoint. The way he said it, Andy knew the schoolmaster wasn't included in that group.

But Andy easily saw through the man's ruse. The schoolmaster was always happy for an excuse to indulge in his favorite pastime—doing nothing for several minutes.

Andy raced out the door of the cabin and to the edge of the dirt road. Immediately he saw his uncle James at the head of the drive. He waved to him. His uncle James waved back.

Andy's brothers and cousins came to stand beside

him, and the remaining students stood just outside the cabin door, showing very little interest in the cattle drive, but enjoying being free of the stuffy interior.

A thick cloud of red dust almost hid the cattle and the drovers as they made their way down the road. Andy knew that if they stayed where they were, they would all soon be enveloped in the dust too, but he didn't care. For those few minutes he could pretend that he was going on the drive with his uncle and older cousins after all.

When Uncle James came abreast of them, he saluted Andy, Hugh, and Robbie, and blew a kiss to his two daughters. Andy returned the salute. His cousins waved to their father and called to him to bring them back something from Charles Town.

With their father gone, Jemima and Louisa moved away from the edge of road, out of the cloud of thick red dust. They were soon followed by Hugh and Robbie, who didn't share Andy's interest in cattle drives.

For just a moment Andy thought about running into the middle of the herd and hiding until they

were so far from the school that his uncle James would have to take him with him to Charles Town. But then he thought about how disappointed his mother would be with him if he did that, so he simply stood there and let the red dust cover his face and his hair, and get into his nostrils so much that it made him sneeze several times.

Finally Edward, George, and Jimmy rode by. Andy waved to them, and they waved back, but almost immediately they were distracted by some steers who thought the school yard was the end of the trip.

Andy continued to stand by the side of the road until the drive had rounded a bend and he could see only the last tendrils of the dust clouds.

As Andy turned to start back toward the school-house, he saw Thomas Rawlins coming toward him. He didn't like Rawlins at all. For one thing, the boy was smart, almost as smart as Andy was, and Rawlins actually enjoyed listening to the schoolmaster read his long, boring poems. For another thing, Rawlins was older than Andy, a little heavier, and was always trying to boss Andy around.

"Jackson! The master said to come back inside!" Rawlins shouted arrogantly. "The Master said you don't know enough to be wasting any more of your time."

Rawlins knew exactly what to say to make Andy lose his temper.

"I know more than you and the master put together!" Andy shouted to him.

"I can say today's poem by heart," Rawlins taunted him. "Can you?"

"What good is that going to do a man?" Andy demanded. "I can read the stories in the Charles Town *Post* about patriots fighting in Massachusetts, and I can do the figures so that we know how much each head of cattle will bring us per pound."

Rawlins snorted. Andy knew Rawlins didn't think much of that.

"I can also throw you!" Andy added for good measure.

Rawlins raised his fists. "Try it!" he said.

Without even thinking about the consequences, Andy raced toward Rawlins and threw himself at him. Rawlins was caught by surprise. He landed on the ground with a whoof as the air rushed out of his lungs. Andy, now on top of him, started pummeling Rawlins about the face.

"You there, Jackson! Stop that!" Andy looked up and saw the schoolmaster standing just outside the cabin door. He had a huge switch in his hand. "Fighting is uncivilized. Which means that you, Jackson, are uncivilized!"

Andy stood up and brushed himself off. He offered Rawlins a hand, which Rawlins took, and pulled him up.

"We weren't fighting," Andy shouted to the schoolmaster. "We were just wrestling."

"Whatever you call it, stop it," the schoolmaster said, "and come inside and finish your work." With that, he disappeared back into the cabin.

"Next time I'll be ready for you, Jackson," Rawlins muttered under his breath, as he headed back to the cabin.

Andy didn't care how much schoolwork he had already missed. He was sure he could catch up in no time.

He walked slowly to the pump just outside the

door. He knew that if he had been on the cattle drive, he wouldn't have to wash off at a pump. He'd join the other drovers as they took their baths in one of the many creeks they passed. That day would come, Andy knew. Then, for the second time that morning, he washed cattle dust off his face.

When school was out that day, Andy headed home with his brothers and cousins. Even though Andy was still disappointed about not getting to go on the cattle drive, he had turned to thinking about what his mother had said to him that morning, that she was going to tell him all about how their family had come to America. It was a story he had heard only in bits and pieces. Now he would hear it all.

Andy and his brothers did their chores, which had almost tripled with the men and older boys gone. But Andy was strong and quite capable and wanted to show his mother and Aunt Jane that he could take care of them.

Finally, with supper over and the dishes out of the way, Mrs. Jackson asked everyone to decide what task they wanted to work on that evening and then to gather together in front of the fireplace in the kitchen, because she was going to tell them a story.

Often when they gathered like this, the different adult family members merely talked, telling about their day, giving their opinions on various matters, including what news was available from passing travelers or what Andy had read to them from the Charles Town newspaper. But tonight was different, Andy knew. He was going to hear his family history.

Usually the girls knitted or worked at the spinning wheel. Most of the time the boys whittled something like wooden pegs or spoons, but Andy decided he didn't want a task to do tonight, because he wanted to direct his entire attention to what his mother was saying.

Andy and his brothers and their cousins always sat on the floor, as near the hearth as they could, enjoying the warmth of the fire. The adults all sat in straight-backed chairs. Aunt Jane, however, always sat in a long seated chair, with her feet on a stool, covered with a blanket. Andy didn't remember a time when his aunt Jane wasn't ill. The rest of the Crawford family was in very good health, but Aunt Jane seemed to grow weaker every day.

Andy realized how fortunate they were. With his father dead, all kinds of horrible things could have happened to his family, including their being separated and sent to live with different relatives. Even though he was sad to see his aunt Jane slowly losing her health, he was just glad that his own mother was healthy and could help to take care of her sister. It was as if his mother were the mother to the Crawford cousins, and Uncle James were the father to the Jackson boys.

With everyone started on his or her task, Mrs. Jackson said, "I promised Andy this morning that I would tell him the story of our family. I hope the rest of you don't mind."

"Oh, no, Aunt Betty!" the Crawford girls said. "We want to hear it too."

Mrs. Jackson gave them all big smiles. "Well, the Jacksons lived in Carrickfergus, in the northern port of Ireland called Ulster, but our forefathers had come from Scotland many years before," she began. "My family's name was Hutchinson, and they were weavers."

Louisa looked up from her spinning wheel. "I'm spinning yard so we can weave things," she said. "Is that what your family did too?"

"I'm sure they did, Louisa," Mrs. Jackson replied. She looked back at Andy, not to ignore the rest of the people in the room, Andy knew, but because she wanted to let him know that this story was really for him. "Your grandfather Jackson owned a store," she continued. "It was a very good store too, and he hoped that his sons would take over for him when he got too old to run it, but none of his boys liked storekeeping.

"Your grandfather didn't know what to think about that. It worried him a lot. Your uncle Sam was a sailor. Your uncle Hugh was a soldier. He helped defeat the French in Canada, and after that he was sent to fight the Cherokees here in the Carolinas."

"What about Father?" Andy asked, trying to hide the impatience in his voice. "What did he do?"

"Andrew farmed," his mother replied, with what Andy thought was a hint of sadness in her voice. "Why he was interested in the land, no one knew, because it was the hardest work of all. It wasn't like here at all, Andy. A man wasn't allowed to buy even an acre for himself. He had to rent it from a rich landowner, most of whom were British, and the rent was so high that it was almost impossible to make a living."

At the mention of the word "British," Andy could feel himself close to losing his temper. Once again he vowed to fight the British when he got old enough.

"When your uncle Hugh came home from America, your father couldn't get enough of his stories about how you could buy all the land you could farm, the land would be yours forever, and you would never have to pay high rent to the British.

"Andy, it was then that your father decided that we were coming to America, to where your uncle Hugh had been, here in the Waxhaws. He said it was like a garden. When I asked him where it got its strange name, he said that it was named for a tribe of Indians that used to live around here. Well, Andy, we expected a paradise on earth."

Mrs. Jackson smiled wanly and closed her eyes for a few minutes. There was no other sound in the kitchen except for the crackling fire in the fireplace.

Andy wondered if his mother had fallen asleep, but then she opened her eyes again and said, "But when we got here, all we found was red soil. It got into our clothes and never came out, no matter how many times they were washed.

"But your father never once complained. He never once suggested that we return home to Ulster. No. He could buy land, Andy. He knew that when he and I were gone, the land would belong to our sons. Your father felt like a king!

"That year we cleared the land and put in a small crop. We even built a cabin. Then the next year we cleared some more land and planted more crops. We added on to the cabin. It was slowly becoming a real home."

Mrs. Jackson paused. "We could not have been happier. We now had two wonderful boys, with another one on the way—that was you, Andy. Our future in America seemed bright.

"But late in the winter of that second year, your father tried to move a tree that he had felled, and he strained himself badly. It wasn't just his back or his arms or legs, no, it was something he did to his insides. He only lived a few days after that, Andy, but before he died, he told me to keep the land for you boys, and I promised him that I always would. We still own that land, about two hundred acres, near Twelve Mile Creek. It's your inheritance."

The Crawford girls had stopped their tasks and were sniffling.

Andy wasn't quite sure how he felt. Once again, he knew that the British had affected his life. If his father hadn't come to America, would he still be alive? he wondered. If he had been able to own land in Ireland instead of having to pay high rent to the British, would he have still wanted to move, even after hearing all of Uncle Hugh's stories? Somehow, Andy felt that his father would have come to America, for the adventure, as well as for the land. Inside, Andy suddenly knew that he was just like his father, and not in name only. He was destined to do things. He wasn't content just to sit still. He wanted to see what was beyond all of the bends in the roads that were being built through the forests and the grasslands of this vast country.

"Are you sure you want to continue, Betty?"

Aunt Jane ventured, breaking the silence that had enveloped the room.

"Yes, Jane. The story isn't over yet," Mrs. Jackson said. She turned to her three sons. "I thought my life was over, but you gave me the strength to go on," she continued. "I knew your father wanted to be buried in a churchyard, that that was very important to him, and even though it was snowing, I left Hugh in charge and walked to our nearest neighbors, the O'Donnels, and asked for their help.

"Mr. O'Donnel made your father's coffin. It was fine looking, boys, from the same cherry wood he had used for their daughter the winter before, after she died from whooping cough. He also built a sled so I could drag the coffin back home. The snow actually made it easier to do. I dressed your father in his best work clothes, put him in the coffin, and then Hugh and Robbie helped me drag the coffin to the churchyard.

"The entire congregation helped us dig your father's grave. The ground was cold, but not frozen. They were all very kind to us. After the funeral, I knew that I would have to make some difficult decisions. I was a widow with two young boys and another child on the way. I knew I couldn't work the farm, but I had two sisters who lived nearby, and they were married to men who were not only prosperous but very kind.

"First we went to your aunt Margaret McKemey's house, where you were born on March 15, 1767, Andy. I now had three wonderful sons. "Still, I was unsure about our future."

"Let me finish the story, Betty," Aunt Jane said.

Andy looked over at his aunt Jane in surprise. Her face was backlit by the crackling fire.

"I had become very sick, and I was quite worried about how I was going to take care of my husband and my children," Aunt Jane said. "It occurred to me that a plan I suddenly conceived could benefit both my family and my sister's." Aunt Jane looked at Andy's mother. "We could not have survived without you, my dear Betty. I shall always be eternally grateful to you."

Mrs. Jackson stood up and walked over to her sister. They put their arms around each other. "God provides," she said.

For a few minutes Andy waited for his mother to continue, and when she didn't, he said, "Is that the end of the story, Mother?"

His mother looked up, tears in her eyes, and said, "Oh, no, Andy, that most certainly is not the end of the story, but you have to live the rest of it yourselves, you and Hugh and Robbie. It was your father who chose America as the setting for your life's story. By letting you know how and why you got here, I thought you might be able to live the rest of your story better."

Andy thought about that for several minutes. It was exciting to think that he was a character in a story about a country that seemed to have so much promise.

"Now, children, it's late," Mrs. Jackson said, "You won't want to get up in the morning if you don't hurry off to bed."

The Crawford house was one of the most comfortable houses in the Waxhaws. It had two rooms on the second floor, one for the boys and one for the girls. There were very few families in the area as fortunate as the Crawfords and the Jacksons.

As Andy headed for the bedroom he shared with his brothers and his cousins, he took a solemn, silent oath. He would live a life in America that would have made his father proud of him.

Wagon Train to Boston!

One morning three weeks later, Andy was with Hugh and Robbie in the loft of the barn, pitching hay down so they could feed the milk cows, when they heard the distant pounding of horses' hooves on the road that went past the Crawford farm.

A crack in the wood gave Andy a good view of the surrounding area, including the south approaches of the road.

"It's Uncle James!" Andy cried. "They're back from Charles Town."

Quickly Andy and his brothers finished pitching down the rest of the hay, then they climbed down themselves and ran toward the house, shouting, "They're back! They're back!"

At that moment the entire household stopped. Andy and his brothers, followed by their Crawford cousins, ran to the road to await the arrival of Uncle James, the older Crawford boys, and the rest of the drovers. Even Aunt Jane stood at the front door with Andy's mother.

Andy's cousins kept speculating on what their father had brought them back from Charles Town, but as soon as Uncle James and the rest of the men reined in, Andy could sense that something was different this time.

After Uncle James had kissed Aunt Jane and hugged the girls, he asked everyone to gather in the kitchen. There was some very important news that he wanted to tell them.

Andy's heart was pounding. What had happened in Charles Town that had excited his uncle so much? he wondered.

He soon found out that it wasn't anything that had happened in Charles Town, but in Massachusetts, many miles to the north.

"Remember when the good people up there got so angry about the high taxes that the British expect us to pay, that they dressed up like Indians and boarded British ships in Boston Harbor and threw cargoes of tea overboard?"

Andy remembered. He had read the stories in the Charles Town newspaper.

"I never did understand that, James." Aunt Jane said. "Think of all that wonderful tea gone to waste in Boston Harbor."

"That was the point, Jane," Mr. Crawford said gently. "They wanted to show the British that they meant business."

"James is right, Jane," Mrs. Jackson said. "By giving up something that was such an important part of daily life, that is, drinking tea, they showed the British that they would be willing to sacrifice to get their message across."

Andy wondered what he'd be willing to give up to run the British out of the country. "Those people in Boston are showing the British who's boss!" he said.

The adults looked at him with surprise. Even though the entire family was in the kitchen, it was unusual for the children to make comments when the adults were discussing matters.

Uncle James grinned at Andy. "You're right, son, they are, but they're paying a price, too."

"How, Father?" Jemima asked.

"Well, not too long after the Boston Tea Party, England closed Boston Harbor. That made it hard for people to get food," Uncle James explained. "This past year has been difficult, but somehow the people in Massachusetts have managed to survive." Uncle James paused and shook his head. "Now, though, things are really bad."

"That's horrible!" Mrs. Jackson exclaimed. "Will the British let them starve to death?"

"There's no telling what the British will do to bring the colonists to their knees," Uncle James said.

"How can we help the people up in Massachusetts?" Andy asked excitedly. "I'd rather fight the British than go to school."

Mrs. Jackson gave him a withering look that deflated the plan beginning to develop in his mind. Andy knew that his mother would probably agree to letting him help in any way, short of quitting school.

"Andy, I want you and the boys to ride over to all of the neighbors," Uncle James said. "Tomorrow we'll butcher a cow and a couple of hogs, and have a great meeting to talk about how we can help our fellow Americans!"

At last Andy had a way to fight the British. He no longer felt as though he was living far away from the important events that were taking place in this country. The northern colonies might be thousands of miles away, but the people of South Carolina felt the same way that the people of Massachusetts, Pennsylvania, and New York felt. They hadn't come to America to make money for the British!

Quickly Andy and his brothers saddled up horses so they could join the older Crawford cousins in spreading the news of the important meeting the next day at the Crawfords' farm.

They decided to ride in pairs, and to contact families within ten miles of their farm. They'd ask their neighbors to contact other families within ten miles of their farms. They figured if they covered fifty miles, they'd have a good number of people who could figure out some way to help the colonists up north.

Andy rode with his cousin Jimmy. At the first two farms they visited, belonging to the Smythes and the Martins, they received a hearty welcome. Jordan Smythe, who was a couple of years older than Andy, wanted to saddle up right then and ride to Boston.

"We'll throw the British out!" he shouted. "We'll kick them all the way back to London Town!"

Andy grinned. "That sounds like a good plan to me," he said.

But when they arrived with their message at the farm belonging to Joseph Lowe, they were met with hostility.

Mr. Lowe was standing on his porch, a musket in his hands. "Get off my property, you rebels!" he shouted. "I owe my allegiance to the king!"

Andy couldn't contain his anger. "What's wrong with you, sir?" he demanded. "I owe my allegiance only to my Maker!"

Mr. Lowe aimed the musket above their heads

and fired. Andy actually felt the bullet whizzing by him.

"Are you crazy?" Andy demanded. His horse reared, almost throwing him.

Andy and Jimmy backed their horses away from Mr. Lowe's porch, staying close to a grove of trees and hoping that if they needed to take cover, this might help.

"Are you saying you won't help your fellow Americans, then?" Jimmy demanded. "Are you saying you're yellow?"

Mr. Lowe's answer was to let loose another volley of shots, which splintered some of the bark on the trees around them.

"We're wasting our time here," Andy said. "Let's leave before he takes dead aim at us."

"That's a good idea," Jimmy said.

Together they backed their horses into the copse, keeping an eye on Mr. Lowe's musket, which now seemed to be aimed straight at their hearts, until they had almost reached the road and felt they could turn and gallop out of sight.

For several minutes, Andy thought he could

almost feel a bullet speeding toward the center of his back. The idea sent chills up his spine. He and Jimmy didn't stop until they had returned to the Crawfords' farm.

Uncle James and his brother Robert, whom Andy, Hugh, and Robbie called uncle too, were waiting for them in the barn.

When Andy told them what had happened, Uncle Robert spat on the ground and said, "When we send the British back home, we'll send the Tories with them!"

Andy had heard that word before, but he had never really stopped to ask what it meant. "What's a Tory?" he said.

"The worst kind of American," Uncle James said. "He owes his allegiance to the king."

"That's exactly what Mr. Lowe said," Jimmy told them.

"We have to watch those people closely," Uncle James said. "They will betray us. You mark my word."

Over the next hour the rest of the riders returned, telling their stories of success and failure. Most of the people they contacted planned to come, but some, like Mr. Lowe, called the Crawfords traitors and said that they should be shot.

Until that moment Andy had never really thought about the people in the Waxhaws feeling that way. He just assumed that if you were an American, your loyalty would be to this country and all its promise. He never thought that people would come here to live, in order to have the same type of life they could have had if they had stayed in England.

But there wasn't time to think about that. There was too much work to be done to get ready for the men and women who believed what the Crawfords and the Jacksons believed: The British had no right to tell the colonists how to live their lives.

People started arriving early the next morning. Andy thought it was a sight to behold. He almost wished Mr. Lowe would ride by at that moment. Maybe he'd change his mind about being a Tory if he saw how many people supported the colonists. Of course, Andy decided, Mr. Lowe would probably take his musket and fire at them.

Throughout the morning Andy wandered among the crowds of men and women.

"I can send them cattle and corn!" one man said.

That suggestion was seconded by several other men.

"I don't have any cattle or corn," another man said, "but I've sure got plenty of barley. I can send a lot of that."

Some of the women were already planning to send their chickens and some of the vegetables they had put up from the previous summer.

Some of the men were ready to do battle with the British right then, and Andy found himself drawn to them.

"We Carolinians are not the sort to take things lying down," one man shouted. "If those people up in Boston fight, then we'll fight too!"

"Now just who is this we're going to fight?" another man countered. "There's nobody around these parts to fight."

"What about the Tories?" Andy put in. "Mr. Joseph Lowe almost shot me and my cousin."

The men stopped talking and looked at Andy as

if he had just dropped down from the moon.

"What sort of fight would that be, young'un?" one man said. "We're talking about the redcoats here."

"There'll be plenty of time to take care of the Tories after we rid this country of the British," another man said.

The talking and the arguing went on for several more hours, then Uncle James called everyone together. Standing on the front porch of the farm-house, he announced, "The port of Boston has been closed by the British, so we can't send anything by ship, but we have promises of fifty wagons and drivers to carry the food, along with enough men to herd over one hundred head of cattle."

The crowd cheered.

Andy felt proud to have been a part of the day's gathering. The men were right. There were no British in the Waxhaws that they could fight, and make no mistake about it, Andy promised himself, if there had been, he would have fought them tooth and nail, school or no school. But the people of the Carolinas could certainly do something about keeping the people in Boston fed, so they would be strong enough to throw the British out of this country.

Over the next few weeks, Andy thought about the wagon train of cattle and food, as it headed north to Boston. He tried to picture it in his mind as it passed through Virginia, Maryland, Pennsylvania, New Jersey, and New York. He knew it was a long way to go, but he knew too, that the Carolinians were doing the right thing. He was sure the patriotic citizens of Boston would think well of their American cousins in the southern colonies.

It seemed to Andy that more and more people came to the Crawford farm to visit and talk about the war. Andy always made sure he was around to listen. He was fascinated by the details of war.

"Let's play war!" was now what Andy shouted to his brothers and cousins, after they had finished their chores.

Although Andy was still one of the youngest of the combined Crawford and Jackson families, he was always the leader in the war games. Frankly, not having Andy in this position never occurred to anyone!

It was Andy's idea for them all to drill with sticks that he had whittled into the shape of muskets.

"These look like the real things," his cousins told him. "I bet they'd scare the British silly."

Andy was proud of his whittling ability and agreed with them.

When they weren't marching, they were training in other ways to be soldiers, which to Andy meant that they all had to wrestle and race each other around the farm on foot.

"We have to be stronger and more fit than the British," Andy told them. "When the British see us coming, they'll run, so we have to run faster than they can!"

"When we catch them, we'll wrestle them to the ground and tie them up," Hugh said.

"Then we'll dump 'em all on a ship and send it back to England," Robbie said.

Everyone except Andy cheered that idea.

Andy wasn't quite sure he wanted to waste that much energy on a British soldier. Unshouldering his musket, he took aim and pretended to fire, wishing a redcoat were on the receiving end of the bullet. That's how he'd like to send them back to England, he decided.

Slowly things seemed to get back to normal in the Waxhaws. The excitement of the wagon train to Boston died down and although the Charles Town newspaper had news about the war, several months old that it was, and although the men who visited the Crawford farm still talked about it, it began to seem farther and farther away.

Even the war games that Andy and his brothers and cousins played had lost some of their intensity.

Later that same year, Uncle James, with the blessings of Andy's mother, suggested that Andy be sent to a better school, an academy conducted by Dr. William Humphries. Mrs. Jackson still had hopes of Andy's becoming a Presbyterian minister. True to his word that he would help rear Mrs. Jackson's sons as if they were his own, Uncle James paid the entire tuition. Although the school was just fifteen miles from the Crawfords' farm, Mr. Jackson made arrangements for Andy to board with Dr. Humphries. This was normally done only for boys who came from longer distances, but Andy's mother wanted to make sure that Andy was never late to class!

"I wish you weren't going away," Louisa and Jemima told him after dinner on the evening before his departure.

"It's not that far," he told the girls, "and when I come home I can teach you all the things that I have learned."

Frankly Andy was surprised he wasn't more upset about going away. *At least,* he thought, *I'll get to see some more of the world.*

There were moments when he thought that he must be special after all, because Hugh and Robert would not be going with him. They would continue their education under the boring and ill-prepared schoolmaster in the stuffy little cabin near the Crawfords' home.

On the first day of class at the academy, Andy was prepared to treat Dr. Humphries with the same disdain he had given the schoolmaster, but Dr. Humphries disarmed him right away.

"I want you to look at this map, Andrew," Dr. Humphries said.

Andy took the piece of paper and looked at it. Although he had heard of maps before, he had never actually seen one. This particular map was of the east coast of America.

"Here is where we are," Dr. Humphries said, pointing to the location of his academy, "and here is where your uncle James's farm is."

Andy could feel his heart pounding. The piece of paper, this *map*, seemed almost magical.

With his finger Dr. Humphries traced the journey that the wagon train with the cattle and food had taken to Boston. In his mind's eye, Andy could see it pass through the cities and towns, through the valleys, and across the rivers. Suddenly the map had opened up even more of the world to him. It was as if he, Andrew Jackson, had taken the trip himself.

Of one thing he was sure. One day he would see every place on this map!

On his visits back home Andy once again read the Charles Town newspaper to his family. They wanted to know more about what was happening in the northern colonies, so Andy read the stories to them.

"Here's something about George Washington," Andy said. "He's been made commander in chief and has taken charge of the army."

While several people in the room were talking about how they had actually met George Washington in Pennsylvania during the French and Indian War, Andy was thinking about a time when he himself would take charge of an army. He was sure that day would come.

The Declaration of Independence

"I think I'm getting better at writing," Andy told Dr. Humphries one day, after several grueling hours of copying passages from one of Andy's favorite books, *The Vicar of Wakefield,* by a man named Oliver Goldsmith. "I understand the structure of most sentences now, and I can rewrite them so that they say what I want them to say."

Dr. Humphries patted Andy's shoulder. "I think you are finally beginning to understand the purpose of a good education, Andrew," he said. "I've also noticed a great improvement in your reading ability."

Hearing this surprised Andy. "I already knew

how to read when I came here, Dr. Humphries," he said.

"Well, Andrew, you most certainly knew how to read the common words, but now you seem quite at home with learned words," Dr. Humphries said. "It's very important that you know how to make that distinction, and when and where to use these different vocabularies."

This was news to Andy—that you had to pick and choose words for different people—but he would always remember Dr. Humphries saying this.

One early evening in June of 1776, Uncle Robert, who lived on a nearby farm, rode over to the Crawfords' with the news that the war had finally came to the Carolinas.

Andy, who was home from school, immediately ran to the edge of the road and looked in both directions. Not seeing any redcoats, he hurried back to the gathering on the front porch.

"When will they be here?" he asked breathlessly.

"Oh, they're not coming to the Waxhaws, Andy," Uncle James explained. "The British fleet has laid anchor just outside the entrance to Charles Town Harbor."

"I'm raising a company of volunteers," Uncle Robert said. "We're going to march on Charles Town and help the residents save the city."

Uncle James and the older Crawford boys immediately saddled up. Mrs. Jackson, with a little help from Aunt Jane, but with most of the help coming from the Crawford girls, immediately set about packing bags of food for the men to eat along the way.

"I know this won't last forever," Andy's mother told Uncle James, "but at least you won't be hungry when you get to Charles Town."

"James, we do have relatives there," Aunt Jane reminded him. "They won't let you and the boys starve, I'm sure."

"Don't worry about us," Uncle Robert assured them. "We're going to be with the other forces there. We'll eat what they eat, and we'll be thankful for it."

More than anything, Andy wanted to go with them. Why was it taking him so long to grow up?

he wondered. Would there still be wars by the time he could fight in them?

After the men had left, Andy sat by himself on the porch, thinking about what would be happening all along the road to Charles Town. He remembered the maps that Dr. Humphries had shown him. He could still see the roads and the rivers and the towns between the Waxhaws and the coast.

Through the open front door Andy listened to his mother talking softly to Aunt Jane. In the pauses Andy was sure that he could hear Aunt Jane crying. Why would anyone cry about going to war? he wondered. It was something that men did to keep what was theirs, whether it was this house or the livestock or the freedom his father had found when he came from the north of Ireland to the Waxhaws.

Finally Andy could stand it no more. If he couldn't go with the men to Charles Town, then he could at least have his own war here on the farm.

He called together Hugh and Robbie and the remaining Crawford cousins and convinced them that after the British took Charles Town, they would come north toward the Waxhaws.

"We have to be ready to defend our farm!" Andy declared.

His rousing speech made believers out of everyone and in just a few minutes they were all marching up and down the road in front of the house so they would be ready to drive away the redcoats.

It never occurred to any one of them, so convincing was Andy's reasoning, to ask what would have become of his uncles and his cousins if that happened.

The war games continued for another week, then it was time for Andy to go back to Dr. Humphries and the academy.

Once again Andy was surprised to discover that he didn't mind doing it. Dr. Humphries had shown himself early to be a man Andy could trust, a man who honestly did know more about most things than Andy did.

When Dr. Humphries read his students stories about the exploits of the Roman armies, Andy paid more attention than usual, especially if the stories were in English instead of in the original Latin. It was the military information that appealed to him more than the language.

Andy was back at the farm the weekend when his uncles and his cousins arrived home from Charles Town. He was expecting vivid tales of how they had battled the redcoats, so he was disappointed to learn that the fort at the entrance to Charles Town Harbor was enough to deter the British. The redcoats never landed on South Carolina soil. Still, the stories were exciting, even if they were about other people fighting the British. From various vantage points around the city, such as church steeples and the roofs of relatives' houses, they had watched the cannons at the fort firing on the British ships.

"They didn't think we had it in us," Uncle Robert said. "They thought we'd just give up."

"That's what some of the Tories in Charles Town thought too," Uncle James said. "Some of them were taken prisoner after they were caught trying to row food out to the redcoats."

The more Andy listened to the stories, the more he thought about everything that was involved in fighting a war. It wasn't enough just to practice with muskets and to wrestle and to race, you needed to know about forts and harbors, too. That night, after Uncle Robert had returned to his farm and Uncle James and Edward, George, and Jimmy had retired—glad to finally be sleeping in their own beds—Andy suggested that he and his brothers build a fort. They would place it on the other side of the barn, Andy urged, so they wouldn't disturb anyone who was sleeping, and pretend that it was the fort in Charles Town Harbor. They placed pieces of wood, shaped as much like ships as they could find, on the ground several yards away from the fort. For cannonballs, they used big stones. From the interior of the fort, they would heave the cannonballs toward the British fleet. A direct hit meant that the British ship was damaged so much that it sank.

Right before Mrs. Jackson called them in to bed, they were finally able to sink the entire British fleet.

Soon, once again, it was time for Andy to return to school. His mother had not given up on her dream that Andy would one day become a

Presbyterian minister, but Andy's brothers and cousins could have told Mrs. Jackson that the situation was hopeless.

"You'd be the first Presbyterian minister who could curse a blue streak!" Jimmy told him.

Andy proved him right by using some curse words he had recently learned and hadn't had a chance to use.

Dr. Humphries knew of Mrs. Jackson's dream for Andy, but unlike Andy's mother, he was able to be more objective. In fact he prided himself on discovering what he honestly felt was each student's true direction in life. With Andrew Jackson, he hadn't quite made up his mind what that would be, although he did feel that he was getting close. One thing that Dr. Humphries did know, however, was that Andy would never become a Presbyterian minister!

One morning toward the end of August 1776, as Andy headed toward his history class, he sensed that the day would bring great changes in his life. He wasn't quite sure why he felt that way, but he did. It could have been that one of his classmates had whispered to him last night that he had spied several new maps in the study where Dr. Humphries worked.

Maps were mostly what kept Andy at the academy. He could sit and stare at maps for hours on end and in his mind take trips to all of the places they represented.

Even though his classmate was correct about the new maps, for they were now lying unfolded on a narrow table at the edge of the classroom, what Dr. Humphries seemed to be most excited about was a single piece of paper that he was holding in his hands.

"This came to me this morning by rider from Charles Town. It's the Declaration of Independence!" Dr. Humphries announced. "I want to read it to you, and then I want to hear what you think about it."

Dr. Humphries told them that Thomas Jefferson had been asked by the members of the Continental Congress to write a draft of what would become the Declaration of Independence. Initially Jefferson had wanted John Adams to write it, but Adams had refused, saying that Jefferson could write ten times better than he could. It was Jefferson's draft, with a few amendments made by Benjamin Franklin and John Adams, that was officially adopted by the delegates on July 4, 1776.

After that introduction, Dr. Humphries read the text of the declaration. Even though some of the words were unfamiliar, Andy felt that he understood exactly what it meant. His country, the land that his father came to hoping that he could find a better and freer life for his family, no longer belonged to England.

When Dr. Humphries finished reading, he said, "Do you understand what this means?"

For just a moment there was total silence in the room, then one student said, "I thought we were colonies. Are we now independent states?"

Dr. Humphries nodded.

The idea sent chills through Andy. He had thought about fighting the British with guns and bullets and cannonballs, but this little piece of paper was stronger than any of those. *Words!* Andrew thought. *We defeated the British with* words!

Another student said, "Does this mean that we're finally rid of England? Will the redcoats sail back across the Atlantic and forget us?"

"England has said that it won't accept the Declaration of Independence, but George Washington is already meeting with them," Dr. Humphries said. "The declaration will help the British understand what it is we're fighting for."

Once again Andy regretted that the fighting was so far away. He wondered if the British would ever come to the Carolinas.

When he arrived home on his next visit, he was hoping to tell everyone about the Declaration of Independence, but everyone had already heard about it.

"What good is that piece of paper?" Uncle James demanded one evening. "General Washington and the Continental Army have lost more battles with the British than they've won!"

Over the next few days Andy noticed that more and more people were heading north with large herds of cattle and wagon trains full of food. That's what he wanted to do too, but he had to return to school.

Fortunately he was able to find solace in the maps at the academy, which Andy could look at anytime he wanted and plot out exactly where the Americans were fighting the British. That would have to do until he could actually fight the British himself. That time, he was positive, was not too far off.

The Cattle Drive to Charles Town

In late April of 1778, Andy was feeling lower than low. The previous month he had turned eleven, but nobody had made much of a fuss over it, not even his mother. Oh, she had baked a cake, and that was pretty special, he guessed, because the people of the Waxhaws were still sending food up to the patriots in Massachusetts and the surrounding states, and things like sugar and eggs were not as plentiful as they had been before the war. But to Andy being eleven was almost like being grown-up. He was even beginning to *feel* grown-up—something he wasn't quite sure he understood—so, instead of a cake, he would rather someone had said, "Well, Andrew Jackson, I think you're old enough to shoulder a musket and fight the British."

Sadly, that hadn't happened.

Andy finished his chores halfheartedly and headed to the kitchen for breakfast. This morning he was the last one to be seated, something that usually didn't happen, and he noticed both his mother and Uncle James giving him a stern look. Andy was relieved that neither of them said anything, though, and after Uncle James finished the prayer, he started passing the food around the table.

Andy ate steadily, his head slightly bowed toward his plate, not looking up and not feeling like joining in the conversation.

Finally he finished. He was hoping that Uncle James would excuse everyone before long, because he wanted to go to the loft in the barn, to start what had become his favorite pastime of late when he was home from school: lying hidden in the bales of sweet-smelling hay, chewing on one of the green straws, and thinking about life beyond the Waxhaws.

At last Uncle James tilted his chair back to show that he had finished breakfast.

"Andrew!" he said.

Startled, Andy looked up at his uncle, expecting to see another disapproving look and to hear questions about unfinished chores.

Instead Uncle James said, "You're eleven now, Andy, almost a man, and you're looking healthy, certainly less fat than my boys, although you usually eat twice as much as they do, and you're almost as tall as I am."

What was this all about? Andy wondered. Of course he was healthy and tall. He could outwrestle both of his brothers and all of his cousins, if he had to, and he was definitely taller than any of them.

"Yes, sir," Andy said. He glanced around the kitchen. His mother and the older Crawford cousins looked as though they wanted to laugh about something. Andrew could feel himself getting really angry at them. Why were they making fun of him? he wondered.

"What were you planning to do today?" Uncle James asked.

Andy shrugged. "Just my chores, sir," he replied. He knew he should be learning the Latin grammar that Dr. Humphries had sent home with him, but there was no way he was going to do that. Now, if Dr. Humphries had sent him home with some of the maps, then he would have sat and looked at those for hours on end.

"I know. He's going to lie on the hay in the loft and chew on straw," Louisa said. "That's all he ever does anymore."

Andy frowned at her. "Have you been spying on me?" he demanded.

"Andrew!" Mrs. Jackson cautioned him. "You will not use that tone of voice with anyone!"

"Yes, ma'am," Andy said.

"Well, I have something better for you to do today, Andy," Uncle James said.

Andy looked up at him. "You do?"

Uncle James nodded. "It's something you've been wanting to do for a long time, and I think the time has finally arrived for you to do it."

Andy could feel his heart starting to pound. Suddenly all of the things he had always wanted to do came back to him in such a flurry that he couldn't separate them into single events. Now everything was all jumbled up in his head, and he was beginning to feel tongue-tied.

"There are a lot of things that I'd like to do, sir, but what I want to do is whatever it is that you want done," Andy managed to say.

Uncle James gave him a big grin. So did the older Crawford cousins.

"Well, it's good to hear you say that, Andy," Uncle James said, "because what I want done is for you to join the cattle drive to Charles Town tomorrow."

Andy jumped up from his chair. "Do you really mean that, Uncle James?" he cried. "Do you really think I'm old enough to go with you?"

"I do, Andy," Uncle James assured him. He raised his eyebrow. "You may have to give up lying on the hay and chewing on straw today, though, because there are a lot of things to do to get ready for a cattle drive."

Andy blushed. "I only do that from time to time, Uncle James, when I want to think about important things," he said.

"Well, Andy, the important thing to think about today is the cattle drive and what you'll need when we get to Charles Town," Uncle James said.

"Yes, sir!" Andy said.

While Andy and his brothers and the younger Crawford cousins finished their morning chores, Mrs. Jackson packed the things that Andy would need for the trip. It wouldn't be much, but it did include a clean set of clothes to wear while they were seeing the sights of Charles Town.

Andrew's brother Hugh would be going too, but Robbie wouldn't. Robbie was more interested in the land and was talking about farming when he came of age.

Hugh had already been on a couple of cattle drives while Andy was away at school, but Hugh's stories never seemed to include anything that sounded exciting. Andy knew that a cattle drive and a stay in Charles Town would be much more interesting to him than it probably was to Hugh. Hugh was a good brother, but Hugh seemed kind of slow about some things, Andy thought.

Around midmorning Andy remembered something else he needed to do. "I'd better ride over and tell Dr. Humphries that I won't be coming to school for a few days," he told his mother.

Andy could tell that his mother was bothered by the fact that he would be missing school. She was probably wondering, he thought, if his being gone would hurt his work or make him less interested in studying with Dr. Humphries.

So when his mother reluctantly said, "Yes, you most certainly need to do that," Andy dashed out of the house before she could change her mind and say, "Well, perhaps going on this cattle drive isn't such a good idea after all, Andy. If you're going to be a good Presbyterian minister, you need to stay in school!"

Dr. Humphries understood when Andy told him about the cattle drive. In fact, Dr. Humphries got out one of his maps of South Carolina so Andy could take another look at how they would be traveling between the Waxhaws and Charles Town.

With Dr. Humphries, Andy tried to keep from sounding too excited about missing school in order to go on the cattle drive, but once he was out of his teacher's presence and among the other boys, who were returning for class, he couldn't help bragging about it.

Most of his classmates were happy for him since going on a cattle drive was of no interest to them whatsoever. But one boy, Jacob Rutherford, who Andy was sure weighed twice as much as he did even though he wasn't as tall, seemed annoyed.

"What's so important about going on a cattle drive, Jackson?" Rutherford demanded. "We hire men to do that for us. It's low class. Does that mean you're low class too?"

Andy had never really cared for Jacob Rutherford. Until now, they had more or less left each other alone, although their dislike for each other had been simmering just below the surface for some time. Andy had heard that the Rutherfords were Tories. In fact, Andy suddenly remembered that Jacob Rutherford didn't have much to say about the Declaration of Independence after Dr. Humphries had read it to them.

"There's nothing lower than a Tory, Rutherford," Andrew said to him. "That's what—"

Before Andy could finish his sentence, Rutherford rushed at him, catching Andy by surprise, and had him on the ground before Andy realized what had happened to him.

Rutherford pummeled Andy's face for a few seconds, then rubbed it in the red dirt. He stood up and said, "Now, you're all ready for the cattle drive, Jackson. You look just like the rest of those low-class drovers."

Some of Andy's classmates started laughing, and a few of them even clapped Rutherford on the back.

Andy slowly stood up. He pushed away a couple of hands stretched out to help him. He'd take care of this himself, he thought. He didn't need anybody else.

Rutherford's back was to him when Andy finally made it back on his feet. Andy called his name and Rutherford turned around.

"What's the matter, Jackson?" Rutherford taunted him. "Have you not had enough?"

"Nope!" Andy said.

With that, Andy rushed at Rutherford's stomach, but Rutherford was too quick and jumped out of the way, causing Andy to land facedown in the red dirt.

Around him he could hear more laughter and the taunts now of the rest of his classmates. Andy lifted his face out of the dirt, spat several times, and then stood up again.

"Do you give up, Jackson?" Rutherford demanded.

Andy answered him with another charge, this time connecting with Rutherford's stomach. Rutherford fell to the ground with a loud thud, and Andy felt the boy's hot breath on his face as it rushed out of his lungs.

Andy let loose with his fists, pounding Rutherford's face until blood was spurting from the boy's nose.

"Stop it! Stop it!" Rutherford gasped. "You're killing me!"

Andy stopped hitting Rutherford, but he grabbed him by his shirt collar and pulled his face within an inch of his own.

"Say you're sorry," Andy demanded.

"I'm sorry," Rutherford managed to say.

"Say you're a dirty Tory, too!" Andy said.

"I'm a dirty Tory," Rutherford whispered.

"Louder!" Andy shouted.

"I'm a dirty Tory!" Rutherford cried.

Andy let go of Rutherford's collar and stood up. He dusted himself off, got on his horse, and rode back to the Crawford farm.

"What in heaven's name happened to you?" his mother demanded when she saw him.

"I had a fight with a dirty Tory," Andy told her.

Mrs. Jackson let out a heavy sigh. "Well, wash up as best you can, Andy, and then go out to the cattle pens to help your uncle James. He was asking for you earlier. The men are already separating the cattle for the drive."

Andy ran out of the house to the water pump and and worked it furiously until there was a steady enough stream that he could stick his head underneath it. Silently he began cursing Jacob Rutherford for drawing him into a fight that had made him late getting back. If his tardiness caused any problems with his uncle James—if, for instance, his uncle James told him that he was no longer going on the cattle drive—Andy had already decided that he'd get back on his horse, ride over to the academy, and give Jacob Rutherford a sound pummeling right there in the classroom. If it got him thrown out of school, he wouldn't care, for it would be worth it.

As it turned out, however, no one said a thing about his having not been around earlier. As soon as he got to the pens, several of the drovers told him what was needed, and Andy set about doing it.

The next morning at sun up, the cattle that had been separated for the drive were let out, and the drovers, Andrew Jackson among them, herded the cattle onto the road for the journey to Charles Town.

Uncle James and Uncle Robert were in the lead as usual, because they were the most experienced drovers. The rest of the men who had worked for them for several years were right behind. Andrew's older Crawford cousins, Edward, George, and Jimmy, and his brother Hugh rode the sides of the herd, watching for strays.

Andrew rode where all beginners started, at the end of the herd, where the dust from the road constantly swirled around him, as he tried to keep the stragglers with the rest of the cattle. It didn't matter to Andrew that the red soil was getting caked on him. He had never in his entire life been so happy.

Once, when a really contrary bull decided that he wasn't interested in going to Charles Town with the herd after all and headed off into the woods that bordered the road, Andrew galloped after him and within minutes had the bull back in the herd. He delighted in the cheers of the other men. He knew that he was doing a fine job on his first cattle drive.

From time to time Uncle James would ride to the rear of the herd to check to see how he was doing. He always had praise for Andy.

"I think I could herd cattle for the rest of my life, Uncle James," Andy said.

"Well, Andy, I know the first few times are exciting, but I think after you've done this for a while, it'll be just like any other chore," Uncle James said. "You'll do it because it needs to be done, but you'll be just as happy when you've finished it."

Andy really wasn't sure that was the case with him, but he didn't say anything.

"The only thing about a cattle drive that everyone still enjoys, Andy, is the evenings in camp," Uncle James added. "I never get tired of sleeping out under the stars by a fire, listening to the sounds of the night."

"I don't think I will either, Uncle James," Andy admitted.

The road they were on, sometimes little more than a narrow trail, was one of the busier ones in South Carolina. It was important to make sure that the cattle stayed in a long, straight line as much as possible, so that other travelers, on their way north, could pass. When these travelers reached Andy, he always lifted his hat in greeting.

"We'll be stopping soon, Andy. There's a creek just up the road that I think you'll enjoy," Uncle James told him on one of his trips back to the rear of the herd. "The water is sweet to drink, and downstream there's a pool that'll wash all that red dirt off of you."

When they finally reached the creek, Andy was amazed at what he saw. It was one of the most beautiful places imaginable. Andy jumped off his horse and headed for the water. He couldn't believe how thirsty he was.

"Andy!"

"What's wrong?" he said.

"First we settle the cattle to grazing, and then we drink," Jimmy told him.

Andy felt embarrassed. Until that moment, he had been doing what the other men were doing, but now they'd probably think that he was still just a kid after all.

"I'm thirsty too, Andy, we all are, but the cattle need to eat," Jimmy explained to him, "and we've got to make sure they don't lose any weight before we get to Charles Town, or we won't get as much money for them."

"I'm sorry," Andy said.

Jimmy jumped down from his horse and put his hand on Andy's shoulder. "Don't be sorry. I did the same thing on my first cattle drive too," he said. "Only I did it sooner. You should have heard me whining to Pa about how I was going to die if I didn't drink some water."

Andy looked up and grinned. "Really?"

Jimmy nodded. "Really." He grabbed Andy by the shoulder. "Come on," he said. "Stick with me."

For the next several minutes, Andy helped Jimmy corral the cattle in a meadow just beyond the trees that lined the creek. *No wonder Uncle James likes to stop here,* Andy thought. The meadow had a natural fence of trees and bushes, the only entrance being where they would camp that night.

"The grass is plentiful, and we don't have to worry about any of the cattle straying," Jimmy said. "We always stop here. It's the best place along the road to Charles Town."

The herd seemed to agree, because it took almost no time to settle them in, and then Andy and Jimmy joined the rest of the men in the pooled water, washing the red dirt off themselves and out of their shirts. The rest of their clothes, Andy was told, would just have to wait.

Andy couldn't remember when he had ever felt as clean as he did when he stepped out of the pool and joined Jimmy on a huge rock slab, to let the sun dry them off.

"Ah, this is the life, isn't it?" Jimmy said.

"It sure is," Andy agreed.

Andy knew that Jimmy wasn't really all that much older than he was, but he had been going on cattle drives for several years, so he *seemed* older and certainly more worldly.

"Tell me about Charles Town," Andy said.

"It's hard to describe it, Andy. You'll just have to see Charles Town to believe all of the things that are there," Jimmy said. "It's where I want to live when I leave home."

For some reason Jimmy's remark about leaving home for good made Andy feel strange. He knew it happened, that was the way life was, but now that he was farther from home than he had ever been, the reality of it set in. It was at once exciting and frightening.

When the sun had dried them, they got dressed, except for their shirts, which were still damp, then helped the rest of the men with the evening meal. Afterward they took turns making up stories around the campfire until Uncle James yawned and said, "We need our rest, men! The sun will be up before we know it."

Andy yawned too. He had been ready to fall asleep for some time now, but had forced himself to stay awake, not wanting the other men to think that he was still a child who went to bed earlier than the adults.

Two days later Andy saw Charles Town for the first time. It was even more beautiful than Jimmy had promised. It had real houses, not crude cabins. There were streets, too, not dusty roads or narrow trails. But what impressed Andy the most was the harbor, with all the ships tied up along the wharf or anchored in the distant blue water.

"When we get the cattle settled in the market pens, I'll ask Father if I can show you the town," Jimmy said.

"Do you think he'll let you?" Andy asked. More than anything, he wanted to see everything there was to see in Charles Town. He wanted to take every memory he could back to the Waxhaws with him.

Jimmy nodded. "He'll let us off. Our jobs are really over. Now it's up to Father and Uncle Robert to get the best price for the cattle."

With the cattle bedded down in the market pens, Andy and Jimmy put on their clean shirts and headed toward the center of Charles Town.

Andy thought that the houses were even more beautiful up close. Instead of having to walk on the ground from building to building, the way the people in the Waxhaws did, the people in Charles Town had sidewalks made of wood.

"You'd never get your shoes muddy the way you do in the Waxhaws," Andy observed.

Jimmy nodded.

The sidewalks were full of elegantly dressed men and women, strolling slowly along, talking and laughing with each other and with the people they passed.

"Where are they all going?" Andy asked.

"Nowhere," Jimmy replied. "They're just enjoying the cool air."

Imagine! Andy thought. He had never heard of people who walked around, with no particular place in mind to go. It was amazing.

From time to time carriages drawn by beautiful horses passed them on the streets. Some of the people on the sidewalks would smile and nod or bow to the occupants. The people in the carriages would smile and nod back.

Andy was astonished at how easily they did this. No one seemed flustered or acted as if he or she didn't know what to do. It all seemed so, well, *elegant,* and Andy was surprised at how much this impressed him.

"Someday I'm coming here to Charles Town too, Jimmy," Andy said, "and I'm going to dress like these people do, and I'm going to ride in my carriage, and I'm—"

"I'm coming here too, but not to stroll up and down the street," Jimmy said. He looked around conspiratorially. "There's other stuff I'll be doing, like watching the cockfights. Come on! Let's go find one!"

Andy had heard all about the cockfights in Charles Town from the travelers who passed by the Crawfords' farm. Once, after a particularly vivid description from a man who said he'd won a lot of money the week before, Andy decided to hold his own cockfighting competition by trying to get two of his mother's best roosters to fight. The only thing Andy won was a scolding from Mrs. Jackson!

When he and Jimmy finally found a cockpit, it was nothing like Andy had pictured. There were scores of men crowded around the pits, calling out their bets, shouting encouragement to the cocks they had bet on. The cocks themselves, which Andy knew had been bred to fight to the death, were incredibly beautiful birds.

Andy was mesmerized by what he was witnessing. But as darkness descended on the area of Charles Town where the pits were located, Jimmy said, "We have to go or Pa will be thinking something happened to us, Andy. He doesn't really like for me to spend a lot of time in this part of town."

Andy nodded, but was unable to take his eyes off the fights.

Finally Jimmy took him by the arm and said, "We'll be here for a week, at least, because that's how long it takes to sell the cattle. We'll come back again."

But when they got back to the pens, Uncle James told them that he had already sold the cattle at a very good price, because of the war.

"You mean war is good for us?" Andy asked.

Uncle James nodded. "The war is good for the farmers, because the soldiers have to be fed," he said.

Andy marveled at how strange the world was. To the people who were dying, the war was bad, but to the people who had things to sell—things that the armies needed—the war was good.

With the cattle sold, there was no reason to stay in Charles Town. Andy had hoped they would be there longer, for he wanted to see the elegant people again. He also wanted to see more cock-fights. But he had experienced enough of what it would be like to live in a city like Charles Town to believe he might never again be satisfied living in the Waxhaws.

War Comes to the Waxhaws

In the autumn of 1778, the fighting in the northern part of the United States practically ceased as the war reached a stalemate. George Washington refused to surrender, so the British turned their efforts toward the South.

Just before the end of that year, the British took Savannah, Georgia, on the coast, and then began to move into the other settled parts of the state.

In June of 1779, the Jackson family suffered its first casualty of the war. Robert Crawford again raised a company of men from the Waxhaws for the defense of South Carolina, and Hugh Jackson and Jimmy Crawford joined him. At the Battle of Stono

Ferry, near Charles Town, Hugh died of heatstroke brought on by exhaustion. He was buried in an unmarked grave.

The rest of the men helped to save Charles Town once again, but this time, at a terrible cost. In addition to Andy's brother, many others died.

Andy learned the news from a rider who stopped at the academy of Dr. Humphries for water and something to eat. Immediately he rushed home. His mother had also heard the news, from another rider. She was sitting with Aunt Jane in the darkened kitchen. When Andy put his arms around her, he thought she barely seemed to know he was there.

Without saying anything, he pulled up another chair and sat beside his mother until dawn, when she rose and said in a strong voice, "Hugh is gone from us, Andy, but there is still work to be done!" With that, she began cooking food for the people she knew would be dropping by that day to pay their respects.

For a few days things seemed to be turned upside down. Andy didn't return to the academy, preferring instead to be near his mother. From time to time, when he heard horses outside, he would rush to the door, or, if he was in the loft of the barn, look through the cracks, hoping that he would see Hugh riding up with stories about how he and Jimmy had routed the redcoats.

That never happened of course. Andy noticed that now he wanted to be around Robbie more. Despite their differences, they began to grow closer.

"It's just us now," Andy told him, "and we have to keep our family together."

Robbie nodded.

Riders continued to arrive with more bad news, sometimes three or four of them a day.

In February of 1780, the British landed near Charles Town and spent the next few months building their forces to around ten thousand men. The American forces, including Robert Crawford and the rest of the men from the Waxhaws, were completely outnumbered. On May 12, General Benjamin Lincoln surrendered the city and disbanded his army of nearly five thousand men, with all its weapons and equipment and ammunition.

Within hours the British began moving into the

rest of South Carolina. No one opposed them.

On May 29, at three o'clock in the afternoon, the British reached the Waxhaws. Andy was back at the academy.

Dr. Humphries was reading from a Latin book when his wife, paler than Andy had ever seen her, rushed into the room, and cried, "They're here! The British are here!"

For a split second Andy thought he was dreaming. It was actually a scene that had played over and over in his head, since he first read about the Boston Tea Party. Now that it was finally happening, Andy knew only one thing. He had to get back to the Crawford farm as quickly as possible.

"Gentlemen! You must leave at once!" Dr. Humphries said. "Forget about your things. My wife and I will hide what we can. You must now think only of returning to your families."

The students rushed to the stable, where a couple of men who worked for Dr. Humphries had every horse saddled. Within minutes the students were galloping in every direction across the countryside toward their homes.

The Crawford farm was north of the school, so Andy didn't think he'd meet any redcoats along the way, but he decided to use a trail that paralleled the main road. Very few people outside the Waxhaws knew about it. Andy had only ridden a couple of miles when he heard a rider coming in the opposite direction.

Andy immediately reined up and hid in a grove of trees. In a few minutes, Robbie raced by. When Andy realized who it was, he immediately struck out after him.

"Robbie! Robbie!" Andy shouted. But he couldn't make himself heard over the pounding hooves.

Andy pushed his horse harder, knowing that only by overtaking Robbie would he be able to keep him from heading right into the oncoming British forces.

Finally Robbie glanced around, saw Andy, and quickly pulled up.

"I came to get you!" Robbie said. "We didn't know if you had heard the news or not!"

Andy nodded. "Quick! We need to get back to the farm!"

They turned their horses around and headed back

toward the Crawfords' farm. But they had only gone a couple of miles when they heard gunfire.

Andy and his brother quickly dismounted and tied up their horses, then they crawled on their stomachs through the thick underbrush until they could see the main road that went from Camden, South Carolina, to Charlotte, North Carolina.

"It's the British!" Robbie whispered.

What Andy witnessed that afternoon would stay with him for the rest of his life. He watched helplessly as British soldiers, their bayonets raised, ran toward a small group of Continental soldiers who were waving a white flag of surrender and pleading with the British to spare their lives.

Robbie hid his head. "Andy, I can't watch! I can't watch!"

But Andy didn't take his eyes off what was happening. Some of the British soldiers were close enough that he could see their faces, and he wanted to be able to remember them, in case he ever came upon them himself in a later battle.

Andy could see that his uncles were not among the soldiers the British were attacking. In fact he

didn't recognize any of the men, which meant they were either from other parts of South Carolina or from other states.

Still, inside him, his anger was near the boiling point. Even if these weren't Waxhaws men the British were slaughtering, they were still Americans. Andy grabbed a thick branch and held on as tightly as he could, to keep himself from running out onto the battlefield. He knew that it was a losing cause, that he would be shot or bayoneted through the heart, leaving his mother and Robbie alone. He couldn't do that to them. He would wait until he had a well thought-out plan that would rid this country of the British forever.

Finally, as the sun began to set, the fighting stopped, but Andy and Robbie could still hear the cries of the wounded, pleading for help. The British soldiers departed, for what location, Andy wasn't sure, but he and Robbie remained hidden for another hour until darkness had totally enveloped them.

They were just about to leave when they heard voices coming from the battlefield. Some of the voices had familiar rings to them.

"It's Mother, I'm sure of it," Robbie whispered.

Andy listened carefully. Many of the voices belonged to women, he could tell, but now there were so many of them it was hard to distinguish whether or not his mother was among them.

All at once lantern lights began to appear, swinging to and fro in the darkness, and finally Andy realized that whoever these people were, they had come to see if there were any survivors.

"I think it's safe to show ourselves, Robbie," Andy said. "We need to help them."

Andy and Robbie untied their horses and led them into the meadow.

"First we'll let them know who we are," Andy whispered. "If we don't, they may think we're British soldiers!"

"That's a good idea," Robbie agreed.

"Hello, there! We're the Jackson boys!" Andy called. "We've come to help!"

For a few moments, all talking in the meadow stopped, then a man called, "Show yourselves!"

Andy and Robbie started walking toward the

nearest lantern. When they reached it, the man who was holding the lantern swung it upward, blinding them, but also illuminating them enough that there were other shouts of "It is them! It is! Mrs. Jackson! Here are your sons!"

Andy heard a muffled cry and in a few seconds their mother had enveloped them in her arms.

"I thought the British had taken you both," she sobbed.

"No, Mother, we knew what to do," Andy told her. "We're all right."

Quickly Andrew told the crowd what he and Robbie had seen, then both boys set about helping the men bury the soldiers the British had butchered. The graves were dug on the spot where the soldiers had died. There were simply too many of them for a proper burial in a churchyard, as was the custom. When they finished, Andy counted 113 graves.

There were also 150 wounded soldiers, some of them in serious condition. After the Waxhaws men fashioned makeshift stretchers out of tree branches from the nearby woods, the soldiers were taken to the Waxhaws Presbyterian Church. Several of the soldiers died on the way and were buried in the churchyard. Mrs. Jackson and the other women nursed the remaining soldiers as best they could. Still, within the next few days, several more soldiers succumbed to their wounds. The ones who did recover were taken in by Waxhaws families until they could make arrangements to return to another army unit, or, in some cases, to return home having seen enough horrors of war to last them several lifetimes.

When the Jackson family finally arrived back at the Crawford farm, Andy knew that he had changed forever. He thought about the war games he had played with his brothers and the Crawford cousins. The drilling with whittled muskets, the wrestling and the chases, the fort they had built at the side of the barn, for firing their rock cannons on pieces of wood that represented British ships—these had been just games. But now all that Andy could think of was the smell of blood as the British soldiers used their bayonets on the pleading Continental soldiers, and the wounded men crying out afterward in misery and pain, wanting nothing more than to see their wives and children one more time before they died.

Andy's hatred for the British grew even stronger. To anyone he saw, from the members of his family to the travelers who passed on the road by the farmhouse, he would demand, "Why do we have to bow to a king who lives across an ocean? Why should we be killed because we don't want to do that?"

No one had an answer to his questions.

Andy's anger grew into a bitter need to revenge what had happened in the Waxhaws. He could think of nothing else. He hardly ate or slept.

With most of the men gone, fighting the British in other parts of South Carolina, or farther south in Georgia, or farther north in North Carolina or Virginia, it was up to the women and boys of the Waxhaws to keep life at home as normal as possible. Andy would never admit to his mother that he didn't mind that Dr. Humphries had closed his academy, but being at home didn't make him happy either. What he wanted most was to be with other Americans, killing British soldiers.

The Crawford farm was still home to three

soldiers recovering from their wounds at the battle Andy and Robbie had witnessed.

After his chores Andy would spend hours with them, listening to them talk about their families back in Virginia, and helping his mother change their bandages and empty their bedpans. In this way Andy felt he was helping the war effort.

When they were alone, Andy would question them about what it was like to be a soldier.

"A good leader makes a good soldier," one of them told him. "We don't have many good leaders yet."

"What about George Washington?" Andy asked. "Isn't he a good leader?"

The three soldiers nodded.

"If George Washington could be everywhere at once, we'd whip the British in just a few days," another soldier said.

"Is he the only good leader we have?" Andy said. He couldn't keep the deep concern out of his voice. "There must be other men who can show us how to get rid of the British!"

"Don't you worry, young'un, they're here," the

third soldier said. "Cream always rises to the top. This country will produce some of the best leaders the world has ever seen."

When Andy told them what he thought a good leader should be, someone with bold ideas who moved his troops swiftly into battle, it prompted one of the soldiers to say, "I'll make sure I remember the name 'Andrew Jackson.' I have a feeling I may be under your command one of these days!"

"Andy!" Robbie had raced up the stairs into the bedroom where Andy was talking to the soldiers. "We have to hide! A rider just came by. The British are only a few miles down the road. They're headed this way. They're killing everyone they see, not just the men, but the women and children, too!"

Quickly Andy and Robbie got the canes that Andy had whittled for the soldiers, and guided them down the stairs to where the rest of the family had gathered in the kitchen.

"I can't leave the house, Betty," Aunt Jane was saying. "I'll never be able to survive in the woods."

"You can't stay here, Jane, not with the British about," Mrs. Jackson said. "We'll carry you, if we have to, but you are coming with us!"

Andy and his mother had already anticipated something like this happening eventually, given the stories they had been hearing recently, so they had bundled up their most prized possessions in sheets, which they had lined up against the wall in the kitchen. Now everyone who could carry one or even two grabbed them. They left the house and headed for the stables, where the boys quickly put saddles and bridles on the remaining horses so that the women could ride, then they headed out through the back pasture toward the woods a couple of miles away.

"We'll stay here until the British leave," Mrs. Jackson told them.

"How will we know when that is?" Jemima asked.

"I can find out," Andy volunteered. "At night I'll slip out of the woods and spy on them."

For much of the summer of 1780, life for the Jacksons and the Crawfords and the rest of the residents of the Waxhaws became a terrible nightmare. Their livestock were stolen, the crops were taken, and some of the people were killed.

True to his word, Andy became their eyes and ears for finding out what the British were up to. When the redcoats seemed to have left the area, the Jacksons and the Crawfords would return to the farmhouse, which, while still standing, had suffered abuse from the British soldiers who had set up camp in it. Still, it was a welcome respite from living in the woods. Then, just as they seemed to be getting their lives back in order, the British returned, and they would have to flee.

As the days went by, Andy and Robbie and a couple of their Crawford cousins got bolder and bolder in their efforts to make life miserable for the British. At night they would sneak back to the farm and leave gates open, so that the next morning it would take the soldiers a couple of hours to round up the horses. Sometimes, during the day, they would scour the woods for egg-eating snakes, then, early in the morning, slip into the hen houses, gather up what eggs they could carry, and put the snakes in the nests to let them feast on the remaining eggs. Sometimes the boys would hide close enough so they could hear the shouts of the soldiers sent to gather the eggs, then listen to their curses when they realized that there wouldn't be any eggs for breakfast that morning.

During the times when the British left the area, Mrs. Jackson would let Andy and Robbie attend the drills and the general assemblies of the local militia. In this way, both Andy and his brother were preparing themselves for the day when they would fight side by side with their relatives and friends in the Waxhaws. When the British returned, the drilling stopped, and everyone fell back to the relative safety of the countryside.

Finally, toward the middle of July, the British seemed to have gone north for good, allowing the Jacksons and the Crawfords to move back into what was left of their farmhouse. It was better than the woods but no longer resembled the beautiful home they had lived in before the arrival of the British soldiers.

When Andy and Robbie had done all they could to help their mother and Aunt Jane get the farmhouse back in order, Andy said, "Robbie and I are going to fight the British, Mother. I don't want to hide out anymore."

Where Andy expected an argument, he got only a tired smile and a sad nod of the head. He realized that his mother was too exhausted to argue. Sadly he realized as well that she had given up on her dream of his becoming a Presbyterian minister.

Over the last few days Andy had heard talk of an encampment of men from the Waxhaws about ten miles to the west of the Crawford farmhouse, in a hard-to-find wooded area, and that the officer in charge was Colonel William Richardson Davie. Uncle James and Uncle Robert were also there, he had learned. This was where Andy and Robbie headed.

It took them two days to reach the camp, because the men had moved twice, but they finally arrived, much to the delight of their uncles, who took them to see Colonel Davie.

"So you lads think you can help us rout the British, is that it?" Davie said.

"Yes, sir," Andy replied.

He quickly gave the colonel an account of their

militia training and how they had created problems at the Crawford farm by leaving gates open and putting snakes in the henhouse.

Davie laughed loudly at that. "I'd never thought about using snakes as a weapon against the British!" he said.

In the end he was impressed enough with both Robbie and Andy that Robbie was accepted as a private and Andy became Colonel Davie's messenger.

"I need a man who knows how to ride and who is familiar with all of the roads and trails in the Waxhaws," Colonel Davie told him. He handed Andy a pistol. "I'm going to give you this and one of my best horses, too."

"Thank you, sir!" Andy said. He was beside himself with joy.

The Battle of Hanging Rock was the first real battle Andy was part of. On August 6, 1780, Andy rode beside Colonel Davie into action. His job was to carry messages and to take care of whatever the troops needed, which he did very well, but he also paid very close attention to what Colonel Davie did.

Colonel Davie seemed to make bold plans but became very cautious when it came time to carry them out. The more Andy observed Colonel William Richardson Davie, the more he realized that one day he wanted to be an officer just like him.

At first the Americans seemed to be winning the Battle of Hanging Rock, but some of them started celebrating too soon by drinking the rum that they had taken from the enemy, and the British took advantage of this. Soon those soldiers who had been drinking heavily fled in all directions, leaving the rest of Davie's troops to the mercy of the British guns.

Although the British were eventually forced back, there were heavy casualties, among them Andy's uncle James.

Andy and Robbie found their uncle lying on the banks of a nearby river, where some of the other soldiers had put him, thinking that he would soon be dead.

"We can't let him die, Robbie," Andy said. "We have to save him for Aunt Jane and our cousins." What Andy didn't say, but what was also in his heart, was that his uncle James was like a father to him. He didn't want to lose another father so soon. "I need to ask Colonel Davie where we're headed next."

He found Colonel Davie tending to the wounds of some of his officers.

Andy saluted him and said, "Sir, our uncle James is still alive. I suggest that my brother take him to our farm, so my mother and my aunt can nurse him back to health. I'll stay here and help you prepare for the next attack."

Colonel Davie shook his head. "What I want is for you and your brother to accompany all of the wounded men back to the Waxhaws."

Andy was stunned. This was not what he expected. "But sir, I think—," he started to say.

But Colonel Davie raised a hand to silence him. "That's an order, Jackson!"

"Yes, sir," Andy replied.

For the next several hours Andy and Robbie helped get the wounded ready for the trip back to the Waxhaws. His disappointment slowly went away, for he knew that he was obeying the command of a man he had come to admire very much.

If Colonel Davie thought this was what Andy needed to do, then this must be what needed to be done. Andy wanted to remember this, for he was sure that in a few years he would be in a similar situation, and he wanted to make certain that the decisions he made then would be approved by the man who had had enough faith in his abilities to give him a horse and a pistol and to let him ride into battle alongside him.

Captured by the British!

Once Andy and Robbie got the wounded men back to the Waxhaws and turned them over to their families, or to families willing to take them in until they were healthy enough to find their own way back home, they were confronted with yet another crisis.

"Your Aunt Jane and I have decided to move the family up to Charlotte, North Carolina, to wait out the war there, because we think we'll be safer in a larger city, and your uncle James will be closer to a hospital," Mrs. Jackson told them. "So you need to start packing your belongings right away. The British may decide to come back, so I do not want to be in this house any longer than I have to."

Andy was stunned. This didn't sound like the mother he had left, before he and Robbie had joined up with Colonel Davie.

"Mother! We can't do that!" Andy protested. "We have to stay in the Waxhaws and fight."

"Who'll lick the redcoats if we go up to Charlotte, Mother?" Robbie said. "We're the only ones left!"

"If you fight, you'll probably get killed," Mrs. Jackson said angrily. "Do you think I want to spend the rest of my days on this earth without my husband *and* my children?"

Andy couldn't think of any answer that would calm his mother's anxiety, but he knew that he wouldn't be able to live with himself if he simply walked away from the war.

For several minutes no one said anything, and a dreadful tension filled the room.

Finally Mrs. Jackson let out a heavy sigh. She walked over to the nearest chair and sat down. "You're right of course, and I know this is what your father would want you to do," she said. "I'm turning into a selfish old woman, thinking only of myself, forgetting what this war is all about." She turned to look at both of them. "If I were a man, I'm sure I would want to do the same thing. Of course you may fight, and you'll go with my blessing, and, I hope, God's, too, for I do believe with all my heart that God is on our side."

Andy and Robbie embraced their mother, clinging to her in a way they hadn't done since they were very small.

That evening Andy and Robbie repacked their belongings, along with as much food as Mrs. Jackson could get them to carry, and the next morning, before the sun was up, they left the Crawford farm in search of the company Uncle Robert now commanded.

Andy's first thought was to stop at Uncle Robert's farm, which was several miles away on Waxhaw Creek, to see if perhaps they could learn where he and his men were. But right before they reached the turnoff that would lead them there, a rider passed with the news that their uncle Robert's house had been taken over by Lord Rawdon, the British commander in chief of the area, and that it was now serving as the enemy headquarters. Uncle Robert's family had fled to a neighbor's house several miles away.

The rider also told them that their uncle Robert was now a major in the army and that if they headed in a more northwesterly direction, they'd probably meet up with him and his men. "You need to be wary of strangers you pass on the road, though," he warned them. "There are still many Tories in the area." With that, he rode off.

"I've heard Uncle James talking, Andy. People will stop you on the road and say, 'Who are you for?'" Robbie said. "It doesn't make any difference if you're a man or a woman or a child. They'll still ask you."

Andy nodded. "I know, Robbie. Our life depends on whether we give the right answer, the Congress or the king."

"How will we know what to say, Andy?" Robbie asked.

Andy could hear the tremor in Robbie's voice. He thought for a minute. "We wouldn't, so that's why I've thought of a plan."

"Tell me," Robbie said. "I don't want us to get shot."

"Well, you know that we Jacksons would always answer 'the Congress,' because we couldn't stomach to say anything else," Andy said, "so I think we have a better chance of reaching Uncle Robert if we're not seen by anybody."

Robbie stared at him for a minute. "What do you mean?"

"We'll follow the road, but we'll stay in the trees at its edge," Andy explained, "and when we hear somebody coming, we'll hide."

"I like that plan," Robbie said.

Andy could see his brother beginning to relax.

"We were in luck, meeting that rider, Andy," Robbie said. "If we had gone to Uncle Robert's farm, it would have been like walking right into a hornet's nest!"

Andy agreed.

Andy preferred to walk through the trees anyway. It was October, and they were having Indian summer in the Waxhaws. The sunshine was warm, but not too warm, and the leaves of the maples and the dogwood had begun to turn red and orange and yellow. It was easy to forget, if Andy tried hard enough or if he sometimes closed his eyes and breathed deeply, that there were men nearby who would shoot them if they gave the wrong answer when asked a question about their loyalty.

For two days they walked through the forest, hiding when people approached, not willing to take a chance on finding out whether it was friend or foe. When they got tired, they would go deeper into the woods, away from the road, and rest under bushes that still had most of their leaves. Usually when they stopped, they would eat some of the food their mother had packed for them, but, not knowing how long the journey to find Uncle Robert would take, they ate it sparingly and mostly filled their stomachs with whatever nuts they came across.

On the third day the weather changed drastically, which was common in autumn in the Waxhaws. A cold rain, driven by a strong wind, stung their faces and stripped the trees and the bushes of most of their leaves. What protection those leaves had given them from people passing on the road was now gone. They were also cold and wet, and by twilight, even though the rain had stopped, Robbie was shivering almost uncontrollably.

"Let's build a fire, Andy," Robbie said. "It'll dry our clothes and warm us up."

"We can't, Robbie," Andy told him. "If some Tories saw it from the road, they'd come see who it was and ask us who we're for, and we Jacksons could never say that we're for the king!"

"You're right, Andy," Robbie said through chattering teeth.

"It's better to be cold than to be killed by the Tories."

Suddenly Andy had an idea. He and Robbie gathered as many large ferns as they could find, then piled them under a bush, so that they could then burrow themselves into them and hopefully sleep warmer than they would otherwise.

It was dark by the time Andy and his brother finished arranging the ferns into what they thought would make a very comfortable bed. Above them, the storm clouds had disappeared, and the stars shone brightly. The moon gave them enough light that they at least could see a few feet in front of them.

Robbie had already burrowed himself into his side of the fern bed, and Andy was just about to join him when he suddenly stopped and looked deeper into the woods. He blinked a couple of times to clear his vision, then looked off to the side, hoping that his peripheral vision would allow him to focus on the object his brain couldn't make him believe he was seeing.

"What's wrong?" Robbie asked.

"I think it's a campfire," Andy whispered.

Robbie unburrowed himself and squatted at the edge of the bush with Andy. "Where?"

Andy pointed through the trees. "See that flickering light, Robbie?" he asked. "I don't know what else it could be but a campfire."

Andy could hear Robbie's teeth chattering again. He was feeling colder too, just thinking about how nice it would be to warm himself at a fire.

"Do you think they're Tories, Andy?" Robbie asked.

"There's no way to know, just by a fire," Andy said. He thought for a minute. "If we were closer, we could listen to what they were saying and perhaps tell by that."

"That's a good idea, Andy," Robbie said. "If they're not Tories, then they might let us share their fire."

"Maybe," Andy said. "It's worth taking a chance, I guess."

They gathered up their belongings, then slowly started toward the light.

"We'll use our army training," Andy whispered to Robbie. "We don't want to let them know we're here until we're sure who they are."

Slowly, stealthily, they slipped from tree to tree, peering out from behind the thick trunks, getting closer and closer to what Andy knew now was definitely a campfire.

They could make out two men sitting by the fire, their shoulders hunched, their hands outstretched, trying to keep warm.

Finally, when they had gone as far as they could without being detected, they stopped and strained to hear what the men were saying.

The men were talking about somebody named John Sevier.

"Who's that?" Robbie whispered.

Andy shook his head. "I never heard of him."

The two men talked about how Sevier was one of the smartest and bravest men in the war, saying things that could have described any soldier they thought was winning a battle, but it was only when the two talked about how Sevier had licked the British, that Andy was sure the men weren't Tories.

"I think we're going to be sleeping around a campfire tonight, Robbie," Andy said. "I think these men are for the Congress, but I guess we need to find out for sure."

Together Andy and Robbie walked slowly out from behind the tree and headed toward the campfire.

"Hello, there!" Andy called in as friendly a voice as he could muster.

The two startled men jumped up, guns in their hands.

Andy swallowed hard. "We heard you talking

about somebody named John Sevier who licked the British at the Battle of King's Mountain," he said, his voice cracking and higher in pitch than his Crawford girl cousins', "so we were wondering who you're for?"

"Look, Seth, it's just a couple of young'uns," one of the men said, putting his gun away. He held out his hand so Andy and Robbie could shake it. "The name's Abraham Stockbridge, and me and Seth Johnson here, well, we're for the Congress," he added.

The man called Seth Johnson lowered his gun, but didn't put it away. "I hope that's who you're for too," he said.

Andy nodded quickly. "All us Jacksons are for the Congress," he said. "My brother and I are trying to reach our uncle, Robert Crawford. We hear he's a major now and is somewhere around these parts with his men." His voice had returned to its normal pitch. "But we've never heard of this John Sevier."

"Well, we can tell you all about John Sevier, and it's something that you need to know, young'uns, but it'll take a while," Stockbridge said. "Take a

118

seat at our fire. You're welcome for the night."

Andy couldn't remember when he had ever heard more welcome words. He and Robbie joined the two men on the other side of the campfire. Immediately he felt its warmth spreading through him.

Stockbridge and Johnson took turns telling them John Sevier's story.

"Most folks know him as Nolichucky Jack, called that because it's the name of the river nearby where his home is," Johnson said. "Abraham here and I, well, we just never call him John Sevier. It's Nolichucky Jack who took care of the British when they thought they'd be smart and cross the mountains to the west.

"Yes, sir, that news didn't set well with Jack and the folks out there," Johnson continued. "They're even more independent minded than us folks east of the mountains. So Jack decided to teach them a lesson.

"He gathered together a thousand men, he did, and dressed them like mountain men and Indians all mixed up together."

"What do you mean?" Andy said.

"Well, they wore buckskin and carried muskets like the mountain men, but they also had tomahawks like the Indians. They didn't want people to think what they were doing had anything to do with politics, because it didn't. They don't care about politics out west. They just care about freedom and fair play, that's all."

"That's the way I feel," Andy said. "I don't want people telling me what to do."

Robbie nodded his agreement.

"Jack heard that the British had set up camp on some mountain top, but he didn't know which one.

"His men told him that it didn't matter to them which one it was, that the British didn't belong on top of any of the mountains, and that if they had to climb to the top of all of them, they would, and then they'd kick every redcoat off!

"They had already climbed to the tops of two mountains and hadn't found any British, but then one night, a mountain woman slipped into their camp and said, 'I hear you're looking for the

British. We'll, I'm for Congress, and I can tell you where they are.'"

"At first Jack thought it might be a trap," Stockbridge continued for Johnson, "but the more he questioned the woman, who said she had sold the British some of her vegetables and chickens, the more she seemed to be genuine and to know what she was talking about, so Jack decided to take a chance on her information.

"She said the British were about three miles from where they were then, on top of King's Mountain, which caused Jack to slap his hand against his forehead and say, 'It'd be just like the British to choose a mountain with a royal name!'

"The woman was able to tell Jack all about the number of men in the British camp, how their tents were set up, and where the sentries were posted. She was positive that Jack and his men could easily beat the redcoats."

Andy couldn't remember when he had ever heard a more exciting story. His only regret was that he was sitting around a campfire listening to it, instead of living it with Nolichucky Jack.

"Jack ordered his men to march up King's Mountain right then and there," Johnson said, "and it wasn't long until they saw everything that the woman had promised them."

Andy jumped up, startling Robbie and the two men.

"What's wrong with you, young'un?" Stockbridge demanded.

"Did Nolichucky Jack and his men kill 'em all?" Andy demanded.

"Well, now, just sit right back down and let me finish my story," Stockbridge said.

Andy did as he was asked.

"The British are an arrogant lot and thought they'd have an easy fight with these mountain men because they had better weapons and were smarter, but the British didn't count on Nolichucky Jack and his men. When Jack's men started firing, the redcoats began dropping like flies. Oh, yes! They cleaned up the camp all right. Finally a white flag went up, and Jack and his men took the rest of the soldiers prisoner."

Andy jumped back up.

"Young'un, do you have ants in your pants?" Stockbridge asked, a grin on his face. "You can't seem to sit still."

"We need to be on our way," Andy informed them.

Robbie gave his brother a puzzled look. "I thought we were going to spend the night by the fire," he said.

Andy shook his head. "We can't delay any longer, Robbie. We have to find Uncle Robert right away. I want to tell him about the Battle of King's Mountain. He may need some good news like this to keep his men from getting discouraged!"

Andy and Robbie thanked the two men for letting them sit by their fire and for telling them the story about Nolichucky Jack.

"We'll go back to the main road, Robbie. It'll be easier to follow at night," Andy said as they started in that direction. "If we don't talk, then nobody who might be on it tonight will know we're there, and if we listen carefully, we'll know that they're approaching before they can see us."

The plan worked. Only once did they have to seek cover in the woods.

The next day they found Uncle Robert and his men. Cousin Thomas was also with them. Whooping and hollering, Andy and Robbie broke into a run.

"Well, if you two aren't a sight for sore eyes," Uncle Robert said.

"Some men told us about the Battle of King's Mountain," Andy said excitedly. "They said Nolichucky Jack and his men beat the British."

"We wanted you to know about it!" Robbie said excitedly.

When Andy finished telling the story, he said, "Does that mean the war is over, Uncle Robert?"

Uncle Robert shook his head. "No, Andy, it's not over yet. There's still a lot to be done, but I reckon the Battle of King's Mountain has probably put the fear of God in the British."

"We want to enlist with you, Uncle Robert," Andy said. "Can we?"

"You sure can. We need all the men we can get," Uncle Robert said. "Go talk to the quartermaster. He'll issue you both a couple of muskets."

For the next several weeks the land beyond the mountains became Andy's home, as he and Robbie did their part, along with Uncle Robert and his men, to try to force the British to leave the area. But Andy soon realized that they were fighting not only the redcoats, but the Tories, too. The men were wet and cold and hungry, but Andy didn't hear any of them complaining, so he and Robbie weren't about to complain either.

The nights were often the best, Andy decided, as they sat around the campfires and talked about Nolichucky Jack and came up with all sorts of plans to get rid of the enemy.

One evening in May 1781, right before dusk, Andy and Robbie were just about to take up their positions for guard duty at the edge of the camp when someone shouted, "The Tories are coming! Muskets at the ready!"

Andy and Robbie took cover behind a tree.

"I see them," Andy whispered.

"What do they look like?" Robbie asked.

"They look just like us on the outside, but on the inside they're rotten to the core," Andy said. He aimed his musket and fired at the approaching men. "I hit one!" he said.

For the next hour Andy and Robbie and the rest of Uncle Robert's men battled with Tories, killing several of them but not losing any of their own men, until it was so dark that the Tories were able to retreat into the woods without being seen.

"We shouldn't have let them escape, men!" Uncle Robert shouted. "We should have captured or killed every last one of them!"

"Maybe they'll be back to attack us again when it gets light," Andy suggested.

"I don't think so, Andy. They're probably on their way to tell the British where we are," Uncle Robert said. "We need to move our camp. We'll head back to the Waxhaws."

Thick storm clouds blotted out any moonlight that would have helped them see their way through the woods, although flashes of lightning from time to time did give them a momentary picture of where they were.

Near dawn they reached a protected meadow that Andy knew was land belonging to a man who had been killed the year before by the British. His wife and their children had returned to Virginia to be nearer her family.

"We're finally back in the Waxhaws," he whispered to Robbie.

They camped there for two days, cleaning their equipment and resting their horses.

On the morning of the third day, two young boys slipped into the camp with the news that a company of British forces would soon be passing by the Waxhaw Presbyterian Church.

"Then that's where we'll make our stand, men!" Uncle Robert shouted.

Andy could feel the excitement surge through him.

Quickly they broke camp and headed for the church. They had only just taken up their positions when the British began passing by on the road.

Uncle Robert had said that he would give the command to fire when the middle of the company was even with the side windows of the church.

Andy was sure he could hear the beating of all the hearts of the men in the little building, but he thought that his was probably beating the loudest.

Finally Uncle Robert shouted, "Fire!"

The immediate result of that order was that several of the British dropped from their horses and the rest began to scatter, but Andy soon realized that these men were too well trained to run away. Within minutes they were firing back, breaking out most of the windows of the church and, with their dead aim, killing and wounding several of Uncle Robert's men.

All around Andy there was confusion. He looked around for Robbie but didn't see him anywhere, and for just a minute had the mind-numbing thought that Robbie had been killed. Just then a bullet whizzed by him, bringing him back to the reality of the moment.

Andy fired a few more shots, then he shouted, "Robbie! Robbie!"

"I'm over here!" Robbie shouted back.

When Andy looked, he saw the reason Robbie had moved. One of the men had taken a shot to the arm and Robbie was wrapping part of his shirt around it.

Andy nodded, then resumed firing until he was out of ammunition. Just as he started to reach for another musket lying beside one of the wounded men, he smelled smoke.

"They've set the church on fire!" Andy shouted. "We've got to get out of here!"

Several of the men went out the front door, firing their muskets as they fled, and were immediately felled by British guns.

There was a back door, Andrew knew, that was close to the woods. As he headed for it he saw Robbie leaving the same way, but he didn't shout at him for fear of calling attention to their escape.

As Andy darted out the door bullets whizzed above his head, then a bullet struck a man to his right, dropping him immediately. Andy finally reached the edge of the trees and kept running.

"There they go!" a couple of the soldiers shouted. "After them!"

Behind him, Andy could hear the soldiers' heavy breathing and he knew that he'd soon be able to lose them. *These redcoats may have better weapons than we do, and they may be better trained, and their uniforms may be pretty to look at,* he decided, *but there's not a one of them who*

can outrun me or my brother in the Waxhaws.

Ahead of him, Andy was sure that he could make out Robbie, and he knew exactly where he was headed. The swamp! He had to laugh. Even if the soldiers made it that far, he knew they'd stop at the edge of the swamp, because they wouldn't want to get their pretty boots dirty!

Finally Andy caught up with his brother.

"Are we the only ones still alive?" Robbie asked.

"I don't think so, but I don't know for sure," Andy said. "When the fire started, things just got confused."

"I know," Robbie agreed. "Everyone just took off in different directions." He looked around. "What do we do now?"

"We stay here in the swamp tonight. It'll be cold, but I'll wager none of those redcoats will come near it," Andy said. "Cousin Edward's house is on the other side of the swamp. We'll head there in the morning."

After a night in which neither of them did more than doze for a couple of minutes, the sun finally came up, finding both boys exhausted and chilled to the bone. The thought of what they might find at their cousin's house warmed them.

The swamp was about a mile wide and by the time they walked up onto dryer land on the other side, they were covered with mire from their waists down.

"We stink!" Robbie said.

"Well, we have smelled better, Robbie, you're right," Andy agreed.

"Do you think Cousin Edward's wife will let us in?" Robbie said.

Andy shrugged. "Well, even if she doesn't," he said, "she won't refuse us some hot food, that I know for sure."

Jenny, Edward's wife, was so happy to see them, that she didn't even pay attention to the fact that they were tracking mire into her house.

"What about Edward?" she asked them anxiously. "Is he still alive?"

Andy had to admit to her that he didn't know. "But Cousin Edward is a good soldier," he said. "I'm sure he's all right."

Those words seemed to calm Jenny somewhat,

and she set about preparing some hot mush for them.

They had just finished eating when they heard horses riding up to the house.

"It's the British!" one of the children shouted.

Andy looked anxiously at Robbie. He knew there was no escape this time.

Prisoners of War

Several British cavalrymen rushed into the Crawfords' kitchen and surrounded them.

"Well, well, look what we have here," the officer in charge said.

Andy took a deep breath and tried to remain calm, but he could hear the rest of the soldiers in other parts of the house, smashing furniture and breaking anything that was made of glass.

Jenny's children huddled around her. Their eyes were full of terror.

"We're looking for Lieutenant Edward Crawford!" the officer shouted at them.

"He's not here," Jenny managed to say in a

trembling voice. "I don't know where he is."

"You'd better be telling the truth," the officer said. "If you're not, if we find the coward hiding on these premises, we'll hang the lot of you!"

Andy jumped up from the table. "She told you he wasn't here," he shouted, "and don't call him a coward. Lieutenant Edward Crawford is braver than any of you redcoats!"

The officer slowly turned his gaze toward Andy, but Andy met it steadily. "Clean my boots!" the officer shouted.

Andy's eyes never wavered. "I may be a prisoner of war, but I will not clean your boots!"

The rest of the soldiers stopped talking among themselves, plunging the room into silence.

It was obvious to Andy that this British officer wasn't used to having *anyone* talk back to him, much less an American boy. His face was turning deeper shades of red by the minute, and it was spreading to his neck and ears. Andy could see the muscles in the officer's throat trying to work, and he knew the man wanted to say something, but nothing was coming out his mouth.

Suddenly the officer withdrew his sword and swung it hard at Andy.

Instinctively Andy raised his arms to protect his face, but the sword still sliced his left wrist all the way to the bone and cut a gash in his head.

Andy staggered backward as the blood spurted from his wounds.

Jenny and the children screamed.

Robbie jumped up from the table to come to Andy's aid, but one of the redcoats grabbed him from behind and restrained him.

Jenny rushed toward Andy, wanting to use her apron to try to stop the flow of blood, but another soldier pulled her away.

"Get some rope and tie him up!" the officer shouted over his shoulder.

Quickly one of the soldiers ran out of the house.

"You can't do that to him, sir!" Jenny said. "He's only a boy, and he's bleeding!"

Andy knew he had blood all over him, but he wished Jenny hadn't called him a boy. He didn't feel like a boy. He felt like what he was, an American soldier!

"He can bleed to death for all I care!" the officer said to her, but this time no one stopped Jenny from grabbing a cloth, tearing it into strips, and binding Andy's wounds as best she could.

Just as Jenny finished, the officer narrowed his eyes at Andy and said, "I think I saw you at the church. You were there, weren't you?"

Andy refused to answer him. He half expected the officer to strike him again with his sword.

Instead the officer turned to Robbie. "You were there, too. Yes, now I remember the both of you." He walked over and stood by Robbie. "I order you to clean my boots," he said.

Andy could see Robbie trying to swallow and knew he was having difficulty. Finally Robbie managed to say, "No. I won't. I'd never clean the boots of a redcoat!"

With almost lightning speed, the officer slammed the blade of his sword against Robbie's skull, sending him tumbling to the floor.

Jenny screamed again.

Andy, struggling to get up, to come to his brother's aid, received a soldier's boot to the stomach, sending him once again to the floor, but he was able to see that the officer's sword hadn't drawn any blood when it struck Robbie. Even so, Robbie lay in a heap on the floor, not moving, although Andy could see that he was still breathing. *Maybe he's just unconscious,* Andy thought, and decided that might be a good thing, because it would mean that the soldiers would probably ignore him now.

Outside Andy heard the sound of more approaching horses, followed by shouting. In just a minute another redcoat rushed into the kitchen. "We've got him, sir," he said to the officer. "We've captured Lieutenant Edward Crawford!"

"Edward!" Jenny cried. "Oh, thank heavens, he's still alive!"

Jenny tried to leave the kitchen, but a couple of the soldiers blocked her way.

Just then, two soldiers came into the kitchen, dragging a wounded Edward Crawford behind them, and dumped him at the feet of the officer.

The officer used his foot to roll Edward over on his back. "Where did you find him?" he said.

"In the swamp," one of the soldiers replied. "His horse had fallen, and he had hit his head."

Jenny broke away from the redcoats who had been restraining her and ran to Edward's side. She began wiping the grime from his face.

The officer turned his attention back to Andrew. "I'm sure a boy like you knows this area very well. You've probably hunted and fished all over the Waxhaws, haven't you?"

Andy stared at the officer but didn't say anything.

The officer walked over and kicked him in the side. "Answer me!"

Andy nodded.

The officer kicked him again. "I don't think I'll tie you up after all, because you're going to do something for me," he said. "Stand up!"

Andy hesitated, only to receive another kick in the side. Slowly he lifted himself off the floor and stood unsteadily, facing the officer.

"There's a man named Thompson who lives around here, a very troublesome character," the officer said. "Do you know him?"

Andy nodded slightly. Of course he knew Mr.

Thompson. He was a great patriot. Andy wondered where this officer's questioning was headed.

"He's responsible for the deaths of several British soldiers," the officer continued. "You're going to take some of my men to Thompson's house, and if you try to mislead them in any way, you'll get all of their swords through your heart at once!"

Andy shivered. He had never known anyone who seemed so cold-hearted as this British officer. His mind had begun to race a mile a minute. He would never be able to live with himself if he took the soldiers to Mr. Thompson's house and the British killed him, but how could he also keep them from doing the same thing to him and to Robbie and his Crawford cousins if he didn't?

The officer turned to three redcoats who had been standing to his right. "Get him out of here! Make him run in front of you!" he shouted. "Kill him instantly if he doesn't do as he's been commanded!"

One of the soldiers pushed Andy toward the door, causing him to stagger, but he managed not to fall. His head had begun to throb, but mercifully the bleeding had stopped due to Jenny's expert binding of his wounds.

When Andy reached the front door, he stopped and looked quickly back at Robbie, who now had begun to stir. But one of the soldiers prodded him with a musket and said, "Start running!"

So Andy started running. The three soldiers mounted their horses and rode at his heels.

Andy's hatred of the British was now at a fever pitch. If there were only something he could do to kill these three soldiers, then maybe he could contact some of the other patriots in the area, circle back to his cousin Edward's house, and kill the rest of the redcoats. But one look over his shoulder at the three grinning men made him realize that they'd like nothing better than to use their swords on him.

Andy decided that he had to forget about killing the British and figure out a way to save Mr. Thompson. Then, suddenly, it all came together. Obviously the British soldiers didn't know that Mr. Thompson lived quite close to Cousin Edward's house, or they would probably have gone there first—at least some of them. There were no real roads in this part of the Waxhaws, just narrow trails and paths crisscrossing each other, so Andy hoped it would be easy to fool the soldiers that they were going the right way—at least for a while. Andy decided to lead them on a roundabout route through a meadow that was just behind Mr. Thompson's house. The route would be short enough that the soldiers wouldn't get suspicious, but long enough that Mr. Thompson, surely alert for the arrival of British soldiers, could probably see them through the woods.

It took all of the strength Andy could muster to implement his plan. Now his head was pounding even more, and he was sure that the wound had reopened, allowing a trickle of blood to flow down his cheek, onto his neck, then under the collar of his shirt, and onto his chest.

Finally, when Andy thought that surely Mr. Thompson would have seen them by now, he headed toward a trail that would lead to the front of Mr. Thompson's house, leaving the barn area, where the horses were kept, out of the soldiers' sight.

As Andy had hoped, Mr. Thompson and his family had seen them coming. When the soldiers entered the house, they found no one there, although they did find the remains of a half-eaten meal on the table, letting Andy know that the Thompsons had been gone only a few minutes.

Andy tried not to meet the eyes of any of the soldiers as they angrily searched every corner of the house, smashing everything in sight, for he was afraid that he might betray to them what he had done.

The trip back to Cousin Edward's house was even more grueling, for the soldiers seemed determined to get back as fast as they could, but Andy knew that he had to lead them back the same way they had come, because if he took the shorter route, then they would know he had tricked them.

When they finally reached the house, Andy ran through the front door, immediately headed for the kitchen, and collapsed on the floor. It seemed to him that no one had moved, which was a good thing. He had dreaded coming back and not finding either Robbie or his cousin Edward, but they were still there too.

The officer ignored Andy and demanded a report from the three soldiers.

"There was no one in the house, sir!" one of the men said. "From the looks of things, the man and his family escaped just before we arrived!"

The officer wheeled around and glowered at Andy. "Stand up, you!" he demanded.

Andy slowly stood up.

The officer was breathing heavily, seeming to search for something to say to him, but instead, he wheeled around and faced the three soldiers who had gone with him to the Thompsons' house. "Take Lieutenant Crawford and these two boys to Camden Prison at once!" he ordered. "They will have nothing to eat and nothing to drink!" He turned back around to Andy. "And this one is to *run* all the way!"

The trip to Camden Prison was mostly a blur for Andy. Indeed, he was forced to run the entire forty miles. His head wound continued to throb so much that he was sure his skull would soon burst open. Added to that, he was hungry and thirsty. He made sure that he looked away whenever any of the soldiers would take a drink of water or pull off a piece of stale bread to chew on. He knew that none of them would take pity on him, and he didn't want them to know that he cared. He would survive this journey, he knew, and he'd be a better patriot for it.

When they finally reached Camden Prison, Andy, Robbie, and Edward were each taken to separate cells on different sides of the prison.

A Tory jailer opened the door of Andy's dark cell, allowing the overpowering smell of human waste to assault his nostrils. The jailer grabbed the collar of Andy's coat and pushed him inside, but for some reason he didn't let go, and then he suddenly pulled Andy back outside the door. "What's a patriot doing with a coat of such fine material?" he demanded. "I think you stole it from a Tory home you heathens ransacked."

"I did no such thing!" Andy said. "My mother made this coat for me!"

"You're a lying scum," the jailer said. "Take it off. I'm repossessing it in the name of the king."

Andy returned the man's stare. "No!" he said without batting an eye.

The jailer shoved him hard up against the wall. "Now, listen to me, and listen good," he hissed, his face within an inch of Andy's, his fetid breath making Andy want to retch. "I can make your time here even more miserable than it will be, if you don't do what I tell you to do."

Andy was sure the man meant it. For his mother's sake and for Robbie's, too, he decided that he'd just have to find another way to survive the dampness of the cell.

Andy took off the coat and handed it to the jailer. Just as he started into the cell, the jailer said, "I want your boots, too."

This time, Andy didn't argue. He pulled off the boots and, without looking at the Tory, dropped them to the floor.

Andy headed for a dark corner of the cell and sat down, drawing his legs up and resting his chin on his knees. The only light came from a small barred window too far up on one wall for him to see out.

Now he was alone with his thoughts. He hoped his mother was safe with Aunt Jane and Uncle James and the girls up in Charlotte. Somehow, Andy knew, he had to survive this night and by morning have figured out a way to locate Robbie and Thomas's cells so they could escape together. Once they were out, they'd try to learn what had happened to Uncle Robert, and then they might just head up to Charlotte, visit with the family, and then take on some more redcoats.

Sometime later someone opened the door and set a jug of water and a chunk of bread inside. Andy slid his back up the wall until he was standing, then walked unsteadily over to the door. The bread was covered with dirt, but he brushed it off as best he could and took a bite. He could taste the grit, but his stomach had been growling almost from the moment he had stepped inside the cell, so he forced himself to chew, and gradually he convinced himself that he had never had bread that tasted this good. There were bugs floating on the top of the water, but Andy skimmed them off with his fingers, then lifted the jug, and drank what was some of the sweetest water he had ever had.

Andy left the jug at the edge of the door, then returned to his corner to think some more about his predicament.

Andy didn't realize he had fallen asleep until he was awakened by a scuffle outside the cell door.

"No! Don't put me in there with them!" a man shouted. "They have the pox!"

Andy drew himself up even tighter at hearing that dreaded word. Nothing brought death faster than the pox . . . and now someone with the disease was going to be sharing a cell with him?

A key was inserted into the lock, his cell was opened by the Tory jailer, and three more prisoners came inside.

The light from outside the cell let him know immediately that two of the men had the pox, for their faces were covered with the red eruptions. The third man, Andy knew, had been crying, for his face was puffy and drawn. He immediately ran to a corner by himself, while the two men with the pox settled in on the opposite side of the cell.

Andy watched his new cellmates for several

minutes, wondering what to say to them, and finally decided to say nothing, at least for the moment.

Andy surprised himself by sleeping through most of the night. He was awakened by the opening of the cell door. Again, someone placed a jug of water and some chunks of bread inside.

Immediately Andy jumped up, before the other prisoners realized what was happening. He grabbed the jug, again skimmed off the bugs floating on the top, and drank, but he drank only a quarter of the water. Then he handed the jug to the man in the corner. "I drank my quarter. You do the same. When you've finished, I'll take it to the two men with the pox."

The man obeyed. When he finished, Andy turned to the other two men, who were huddled together against the opposite wall. "Your lips may not touch this jug," he said. "You will each open your mouth, and I will pour the water slowly into it. If this is not acceptable to you, then I will pour the water onto the floor of the cell."

For a couple of minutes the two men just stared at Andy, probably wondering, Andy was sure, just how old this boy was who was demanding such a thing of them, but finally they nodded their assent. Andy walked slowly over to them. This close, he could tell that the violent red eruptions covered not only their faces but also their hands and feet. He was sure that if they had taken off the rest of their clothes, there wouldn't be a spot of skin the pox didn't cover.

One of the men leaned forward, tilted back his head, and slowly opened his mouth.

Andy poured as carefully as possible, so as not to spill any of the water or to cause the man to choke.

When Andy decided he had given the man his quarter, he righted the jug. The second man leaned forward and did the same. Soon the jug was empty. Andy placed two chunks of bread within reach of the two men, put the jug back by the door, and returned to his corner.

They continued this routine over the next few days, saying very little to each other. Then one morning Andy awakened to find that one of the men with pox had died. After the man's body was dragged out of the cell, Andy started to talk his cell mates.

"He was a patriot," Andy said, "and yet we allowed them to treat him like human garbage."

The man with the pox nodded, but said, "He didn't blame anyone. He told me he would probably have done the same. The name's Charles Mooser, by the way. My home's in Maryland. My friend's name was Paul Ruston, and he lived just down the road from us."

"Andrew Jackson," Andy said. "I'm from the Waxhaws."

Slowly the other man came around too. His name, he told them, was Jacob Cunningham, and he was from Georgia.

After that, the three of them talked about many things, but mostly about how they were going to escape from Camden Prison and what they were going to do to the British soldiers who had put them there. Andy even talked Cunningham into exercising with him in their cell, to keep up their strength.

"You're still a young'un, you are," Cunningham told Andy one day, "but you're a leader of men already. I can tell."

Andy swelled with pride at the comment, and at that moment he vowed to remember what Cunningham had said to him and to make himself worthy of such a remark.

Andy knew that Mooser was getting worse. He had begun to have coughing spasms. He had stopped eating and was now refusing to take any water. Andy pulled a large splinter from one of the wall boards, smoothed one end, and used it to pry open Mooser's lips, so he could let water trickle through his missing teeth into his throat. It was a tricky job, making sure that the water didn't choke the man. Soon, though, Andy was unable to do even that, and he knew it wouldn't be long before Mooser died too.

Then, early one morning, Andy heard a commotion outside his cell.

"Quick, Cunningham, I need to see out!" Andy said.

Cunningham squatted down, facing the wall, and let Andy climb onto his shoulders. Slowly he began to stand up, allowing Andy at last to see out the window.

"I see American soldiers!" he said. "Something's going on!"

Cunningham squatted down again. Andy jumped off his shoulders and ran over to the cell door and put his ear against it. After a few minutes he said, "The Tories are shouting about something, but I can't make it out."

Just then a key was inserted in the lock, and two of the Tory jailers came in. They were carrying a ladder and some boards and nails. Within a few minutes, they had boarded up the small window that Andy had just been looking out.

Andy was totally disheartened. Did this mean that the Americans weren't strong enough to take the prison? he wondered. Was the boarding up of the window meant to keep the patriots from creating a ruckus and becoming a rallying point for the American soldiers?

Andy went to his corner of the cell and sank to the floor. Now he felt alternately hot and cold, but he didn't want to think about what might be the reason for it.

For the rest of the day nobody stirred, not even

to get the water and the bread that was finally brought to them.

By the next morning Andy had an idea. He still felt feverish, but the excitement of the new idea gave him strength. He convinced Cunningham to let him stand on his shoulders again.

When he was finally level with the boards that covered the window, he found what he was looking for: a small knot in the wood. He began working it loose. Several times Cunningham lowered him to the ground in order to rest his shoulders, but on the third trip up to the window, Andy was able to remove the knot of wood and once again look out.

"What do you see this time?" Cunningham said.

"I see soldiers and cannons," Andy said weakly. "They're not too close to us yet, but they're still there." Andy felt himself beginning to black out. "I need down, Cunningham," he managed to say.

Once again Andy huddled in his corner. He couldn't stop shaking. He felt as though he were burning up.

Soon Andy began to lose all sense of time. He couldn't keep his eyes open, and he felt as if he couldn't move. He thought he remembered Cunningham using the smooth splinter to pry open his mouth to give him water, but he wasn't sure if that were really happening or if he were just dreaming.

In his head, too, he thought he could hear his mother's voice. She was calling him. "Andrew Jackson. Show yourself. Show yourself!"

Andy forced himself to open his eyes. When he looked around, he saw that there was no one else inside the cell except him, and the door was standing open. Mooser and Cunningham were gone.

"Show yourself, Andrew Jackson!" the voice called again.

It couldn't be, Andy thought. *This has to be a dream.*

Slowly Andy pushed himself to a standing position and began staggering toward the open door. There were no Tories waiting for him, so he walked outside into the bright sunshine.

His mother was standing just a few feet away from the boarded-up window to his cell. She was holding the reins of two of the worst-looking horses

Andy had ever seen. Robbie was beside her, leaning on her shoulder. Andy was stunned by his brother's appearance. Robbie's face and arms were covered with violent red eruptions. Robbie had the pox!

Andy staggered toward his mother, and she opened her arms to him.

The three of them stood together, feeling each other's warmth, then Andy pulled away.

"Mother, how did you come to be here?" he asked.

"I learned that you and Robbie and Thomas had been taken prisoner," Mrs. Jackson replied. "I was able to get you and Robbie on a list for an exchange. No one seems to know where Thomas is."

For the first time Andy looked around and saw the prisoner exchange taking place. Patriots and soldiers were mingling side by side in the prison. It was a peculiar sight, Andy thought.

"It's called a truce," Mrs. Jackson explained. "It'll last only long enough for the patriots to get our men back and for the British to get theirs, then the killing will start all over again. We have to hurry. Robbie is very ill, and I don't feel safe here."

She nodded to the horses. "Robbie will ride one, and you'll ride the other," she said.

Andy helped Robbie onto one horse, then he held the other one for his mother to get on. His mother started to protest, but Andy said, "I'm not riding it. You are."

Mrs. Jackson didn't argue.

After they had ridden several miles, they came to a creek.

"Let's stop here for water, Andy," Mrs. Jackson said, "and so Robbie can lie on the grass."

Andy could only nod that he agreed with his mother's suggestion. Although he would never have let his mother know it, Andy had been wondering just how much farther he would be able to travel himself. His entire body ached, and he felt as though he were about to collapse.

After making sure his brother was comfortable, Andy spread a cloth on the ground and began helping his mother set out the food that she and Aunt Jane had cooked especially for them.

But when Andy started to stuff chicken and

potatoes and squash into his mouth all at once, his mother said, "Eat slowly, Andy. Your stomach is sure to have shrunk some, and it will make you sick if you try to fill it too fast."

It took tremendous self-control to follow his mother's admonition, but Andy managed to eat a little more slowly.

Robbie, however, ate nothing, and lay still under his blanket. When they were once again on the road, he began to prattle nonsensically. Mrs. Jackson became increasingly anxious about him.

Finally, on the third night after they had left Camden Prison, they reached Charlotte. Most of the last day they had traveled in a cold rain. Robbie was barely conscious, and Andy was now burning up with fever. Earlier that morning he had noticed bright red sores starting to erupt on his skin.

Andy and Robbie were bedded in the carriage house at the rear of the main house. Mrs. Jackson never left their sides, except to get the food and water that Aunt Jane and Uncle James would set outside the door.

On the second day they were back, Robbie died.

Another week passed before Mrs. Jackson gave Andy the news.

"You and I are the only ones of our family left here on this earth, Andy," his mother said. She looked at him with vacant eyes and then turned to stare into space. "Your father, Hugh, and Robbie are all together in heaven, I'm sure, and that will sustain me until I can join them."

At that moment the hatred Andy felt for the British totally consumed him. "Mark my words, Mother," he managed to say. "As God is my witness, I will avenge the deaths of my brothers!"

All Alone

After Robbie's death, Andy, his mother, and Aunt Jane decided to move back to the Waxhaws. Uncle James had fully recovered from his wounds and was again away with the army, as were Uncle Robert and the rest of the Crawford boys who were still alive. All of the Crawford girls were now married. Although they lived nearby, they were busy with their own young children and helping each other with farm chores, since their husbands were away fighting the British.

Andy and his mother found themselves struggling to do even the most mundane activity. The war had taken away their spirit. Sometimes it seemed as though it had also taken away their will to live.

Congress had put General Horatio Gates in charge of a southern army consisting of militia units from all over the South plus some of George Washington's most highly trained Continentals. General Gates had met Lord Cornwallis at Camden hoping for a decisive defeat of the redcoats in South Carolina, but the British forces outmaneuvered him, and Gates was forced to fall back.

A disappointed Congress recalled Gates and let George Washington replace him with General Nathanael Greene, who was considered not only a first-rate officer but a man who was blessed with a lot of common sense, something that had been sorely lacking in Gates.

Slowly but surely, the smaller American forces began to defeat the British forces. In January 1781, at the Battle of Cowpens, in the northwestern part of South Carolina, the Americans defeated Colonel Banastre Tarleton, who was one of Lord Cornwallis's best officers. That was followed by another major victory at Guilford Courthouse, forcing Lord Cornwallis to retreat to the seaport of

Wilmington, North Carolina, where he planned to wait for reinforcements. But Lord Cornwallis soon decided that there was no future in fighting the patriots in the Carolinas, so he decided to push farther north, into Virginia, to join forces with troops under Benedict Arnold, the American traitor who had sold out to the British.

That was the world in which Andrew Jackson found himself in 1781, as he continued his slow recovery from the pox. He was tired and listless, and the drying sores itched constantly. Still, he considered himself fortunate to be alive. Most people never recovered from the disease.

One morning Andy was sitting on the front porch, listening to the birds in the nearby trees, and wondering if they knew anything about the war being played out on the ground below them, when he heard the approach of a rider coming up from the south.

Even though the war had made times hard, it was still the custom to invite riders in to share whatever food and drink there was left in the house. In return, the riders always shared what news they had.

"Now the British are giving Virginia the same thing they gave us," the rider told them. "In fact, that Colonel Tarleton nearly arrested Governor Thomas Jefferson in his own house!"

The summer of 1781 was difficult for the people of the Waxhaws. Even though there was no longer any fighting there, many of the Jacksons' and the Crawfords' neighbors were dead, and most of the surviving men and boys were still away in the army. There was very little food, because there were so few people to grow it. A portion of that food was often sent to the armies, and when they didn't have food to send, the people of the Waxhaws sent seeds, especially kernels of corn. That meant there was nothing left to plant, so it all became a vicious cycle of need.

It seemed to Andy that their farmhouse had been turned into a hospital, too. His mother, and Aunt Jane as best she could, helped nurse the sick and wounded soldiers who, returning from the battles in Virginia, could get no farther than the road in front of Andy's house.

As the soldiers recuperated, Andy questioned

them about the battles they had been in. He wanted to know all of the details. Andy knew he was exhausting the soldiers with his questions, but he felt driven to find out how the different commanders, both American and British, made their battle plans. The soldiers seemed more than willing to give him the information. Often they commented on how quick his mind was, how easily he seemed to assimilate what they told him, and more than one remarked that they were sure one day he would use the information they gave him to win his own battles.

After his conversations with the soldiers, Andy would go out and sit in the shade of one of the big trees in the front yard, and with pointed sticks would re-create in the dirt the battles he had just heard about. Slowly he began to see what would work and what wouldn't work, how battles could be won and how they could be lost. In his mind he would fight the battles again, using his redrawn battle plans, and in the end, the British were always defeated.

✿ ✿ ✿ ✿

One Sunday morning Andy's mother awakened him before dawn—something she used to do before the war so he could get started on his chores, but something she hadn't done since he had returned from Camden Prison.

"It's your Aunt Jane," his mother whispered. "She's gone."

Andy struggled to absorb what his mother had just told him. His mind was suddenly filled with images of Aunt Jane, sitting in her long chair by the kitchen fire, wrapped in a quilt, a smile on her face, as the family ate and laughed and told their daily tales about the antics of their extended family. The war had long ago taken that away, but Andy knew that would be the image of Aunt Jane that he would always carry with him.

"I didn't want her to help me nurse the soldiers who have been coming here, but she insisted," his mother said. "She felt she was finally doing her part for the war effort. So I know that she died happy."

Aunt Jane was buried in the churchyard of the Waxhaws Presbyterian Church two days later. Andy stayed home, at the insistence of his mother.

"Aunt Jane would have understood. She knew you loved her," she said. "It isn't necessary for you to come to her funeral to prove it."

When Mrs. Jackson returned from the church, it was the first time they had lived in the house without a Crawford there with them. It gave Andy a strange feeling.

As the weeks passed Andy gradually began to move around the farm more. Each day he walked just a little farther from the house.

Mrs. Jackson and a couple of the soldiers who were almost fully recuperated tilled a plot of ground behind the barn for a little garden. Andy planted beans and squash and even a couple of rows of corn.

"This summer we'll finally have our own fresh vegetables," he told his mother.

When she didn't say anything, Andy turned to see what was wrong and noticed her studying his face carefully.

"The sores have practically all healed," she said, as though she hadn't even heard what he had said about the garden. "I think you're almost well, Andy."

Something about the way she said it produced a

slight anxiety in Andy, but after a while the feeling went away, as he saw his mother cheerfully washing clothes and baking bread and pies.

Then, early the next morning, his mother awakened him by gently shaking his shoulder.

When Andy opened his eyes and looked into hers, he knew that another major change was about to take place in his life.

"What I'm about to tell you, Andy, I've known for several weeks," his mother said, "but I wanted you to be recovered enough that your worrying about it would not affect your health, and now I think you're at that point."

Andy was finding it hard to breathe. "What is it, Mother?" he asked.

"One evening a rider came here with the news that your Crawford cousins George and Jimmy are in a prison ship in Charles Town Harbor," his mother told him.

Even though Lord Cornwallis had moved his troops out of South Carolina and was now in Virginia fortifying Yorktown, the British still occupied Charles Town.

Andy was stunned at the news about his cousins. He suddenly felt selfish. "You should have told me, Mother! Perhaps I could have recovered more quickly!" he said. In his mind he could still picture George and Jimmy, drilling with him in the front yard with their whittled muskets, as they practiced fighting the British. "Then I could have gone to Charles Town myself to see about them!"

His mother shook her head. "That's exactly why I didn't tell you, Andy," she said. "You are getting well, but you're not yet fully recovered."

"Did Aunt Jane know about George and Jimmy?" Andy asked.

His mother nodded. "I told her right before she died, Andy," she said. "And I promised her that I would go to them and do everything in my power to nurse them back to health until I could get them released."

Andy remembered what his mother had done for Robbie and him at Camden Prison. If anyone could do this, Elizabeth Jackson could, and at that moment Andy could not have been more thankful to have been brought into this world by a woman such as his mother.

"I'm much stronger than you realize, Mother," Andy said. "Anyway, I don't want you to going to Charles Town by yourself."

"I won't be alone, Andy. Mrs. Randle and Mrs. Carter are going with me," Mrs. Jackson said. Andy recognized the names of two neighbor women who were also active in the Waxhaws Presbyterian Church. "They think their boys may be on the prison ship too."

For the rest of that day, as his mother began getting ready for the journey to Charles Town, Andy fought against the onset of an overwhelming depression. How was he going to manage the farm by himself? he wondered. It soon became obvious to him that much of the strength he thought he was regaining was his only because of his mother. He had used her strength as his to help him get through each day. Now his mother would be 160 miles away, among the enemy. Finally the weight became so heavy that Andy could no longer keep silent.

"What will I do without you, Mother?" he finally asked, knowing as he spoke, that he sounded like a spoiled, whining child, not the man and soldier that he prided himself on being. "How can I possibly take care of the farm?"

"There is nothing more that I can tell you, Andy. You will do what you have to do. This is now your responsibility, and you won't fail yourself. You never have," his mother said. "The Crawfords were very good to us. They took us in and provided for us after your father died. It is now our turn to provide for them. You must keep up the farm, so that when your uncle James and your cousins return from the war, they will feel as though they had never left it."

Andy swallowed hard. "I promise you that I will do that, Mother," he said.

His mother took his hand. "You're a good son, Andy, and I couldn't be more proud of you, but it's important to remember all that I've tried to teach you over the years," she said.

"You must always be honest in your dealings with other men. If you have an argument, you must settle it fairly, for your reputation will come from that.

"You must be slow to anger—something I know you're still struggling with—and you must let your anger cool before you make a final decision on anything.

"Friendships are very important, but to have a friend, you must be a friend, and you'll keep your friends by being honest and steadfast with them."

His mother hugged him close to her, then released him, looked into his eyes, and said, "Take care of yourself, my son. I shall love you forever."

They heard horses outside.

"It's Mrs. Randle and Mrs. Carter," his mother said. "It's time for me to leave."

Earlier Andy had helped his mother saddle her horse. He had led the mare around to the front of the house, where they had tied on her few belongings, including medicines, behind the saddle.

"Good morning, ladies," Andy said to the women.

"Good morning, Andy," they said.

"I hope you'll keep us in your prayers," Mrs. Carter added.

"I shall indeed," Andy said, a lump starting to form in his throat. "I shall indeed," he managed to repeat.

172

The three horses were pawing the ground, letting everyone know they were ready for the trip, so Andy's mother gave him one more hug, kissed him on his forehead, and mounted her horse.

The three women rode solemnly away, with Andy watching them from the front yard. Just before his mother disappeared from sight, she turned once more and waved to him.

Andy waved back, this time not caring that tears were streaming down his cheeks. He had never felt so alone in his whole life.

Andy reentered the empty house and sat by himself at the long table in the kitchen that had seen so many joyous meals over the years. He wasn't exactly sure how he felt about all that had happened. One minute he resented his mother's leaving him, convincing himself that she cared more about her nephews than she did her only son. No matter how hard he tried to understand her wanting to take care of her dead sister's sons, he needed her too. The next minute, though, he couldn't have been more proud of her.

Andy stayed by himself for an agonizing six weeks

before he decided that no matter what he had promised his mother, he simply wouldn't be able to live at the Crawford farm by himself. He would still do all he could to make sure that the property was kept up, perhaps even staying overnight once in a while, but it was too painful and too lonely to live in the empty house by himself all the time.

Andy went to see Cousin Edward Crawford, who was now back home with his family after finally being released from Camden Prison, and asked if he could move in with them until he felt stronger, or at least until his mother returned from Charles Town.

"Of course you may, Andy," Jenny told him. "You're family, and Edward and I have never forgotten what you did when the British invaded our home."

Cousin Edward nodded. "You kept Patriot Thompson from being taken prisoner, and I'm quite sure that your fearlessness kept the soldiers from doing more harm than they did."

Andy took several days to move his things to Cousin Edward's house, staying there at night, but returning to the Crawford farm during the day.

Jenny and Edward also had another boarder, a Captain Galbraith, who was in charge of the commissary stores and ammunition for the American army in the Waxhaws. Andy didn't think much of him, for Galbraith seemed rather proud and haughty, but Andy also didn't think that their paths would cross often enough to cause any conflicts.

A few days later, when Andy was back at the Crawford home doing what work he thought he could handle in his weakened state, a rider galloped in from the south.

The rider saw Andy by one of the fences and rode over to him.

"Are you Andrew Jackson?" the rider asked.

Andy nodded.

"I have a message for you from a Mrs. Randle," the rider continued.

Andy suddenly felt himself growing cold and dizzy. He leaned up against the fence to keep from falling. "I know a Mrs. Randle. She accompanied a Mrs. Carter and my mother to Charles Town to see if they could find their sons and my cousins," he managed to say. "They were supposed to be on a prison ship."

The rider took a deep breath. "Mrs. Randle is sorry to have to tell you that your mother died of a fever," he said. "She is buried in an unmarked grave in Charles Town."

For just a moment Andy wanted to lash out at the man. He wanted to pull him from his horse and beat him within an inch of his life for bringing him this awful news, but he managed to control himself.

The rider untied a cloth bundle from behind his saddle and handed it to Andy. "These are her things," he said. "Mrs. Randle wanted to make sure that you got them."

"What about my cousins, George and Jimmy Crawford?" Andy asked. "Are they are still alive?"

"They are alive, but they are still prisoners," the rider said. He pulled on the reins of his horse. "I'm sorry that I must leave you alone with your grief, but I have to be in Charlotte tonight."

Andy nodded his understanding.

After the rider had gone, Andy slowly unwrapped

the cloth bundle. Inside he found a dress and some toiletry items, but the one thing of his mother's that he really wanted, her Bible, wasn't there.

With tears streaming down his face, Andy started walking back to his cousin Edward's house. The only thing that he could think of was that he was now completely alone.

Everyone Is Worried about Andy

Cousin Edward and Jenny comforted Andy as much as they possibly could, and for his part Andy buried himself in all the chores that he could physically handle, both at the Crawford farm and at his cousin Edward's house. Mostly he was able to keep his mind off his mother's death and on making sure that he regained his strength and fulfilled one of her last wishes—that the Crawford farm be in good shape for the time when his uncle James and the cousins who were still alive would return to the Waxhaws.

Slowly, in the late autumn of 1781, Andy felt his life returning to normal, as normal as it would ever be, given that, for all intents and purposes, he was now an orphan.

The only problem that existed for him came in the form of Captain Galbraith. For some inexplicable reason, Andy's presence in his cousin Edward's house created hostility in the man. One evening when Galbraith was later than usual in returning home, Cousin Edward asked Andy if he would take care of the captain's horse so Galbraith could eat his supper hot. Andy, not wanting to seem ungrateful to his cousin, agreed to do it.

Later that evening Galbraith confronted Andy, just as he was about to go to bed. "You scratched my saddle when you were putting it away," he hissed. "You're an imbecile who doesn't know how to handle fine things!"

Andy seethed at the lie. "Your saddle was already scratched, Captain Galbraith. I just assumed that it was you who didn't know how to take care of fine things!"

From that moment on there existed such animosity between the two, that Andy began to spend more and more time at the Crawford farm, and occasionally even at the homes of other cousins in the Waxhaws.

Slowly Andy's strength returned and, with it, a profound change in the way he looked at the world. His friends and family noticed it. He seemed more serious, they said, more willing to listen to what they had to say without flying off the handle. Of course, he told them, everything and everyone in the Waxhaws had changed too, and they all had to admit that that was true.

In October of that year Lord Cornwallis had been defeated at Yorktown. There was talk that the peace papers would not be signed for many months, but the people in the Carolinas, both civilians and soldiers, couldn't wait for that. As soon as the fighting had ended, they moved back to their homes and farms. Tories who had fought against independence from Great Britain found themselves hated and despised. Most of them moved to Canada or back to England.

One morning, just as Andy had finished digging a hole for a new fence post, his uncle James came riding up. For a few moments Andy didn't recognize him, because he had aged a lot, but when Uncle James smiled, Andy would have recognized him anywhere.

"Welcome home, Uncle James," Andy said.

"Thank you, Andy," Uncle James said. "I am genuinely glad to be back and to see you."

Andy knew that Uncle James had been told about Aunt Jane's death by riders who had come by the farm and were on their way to the battle-front, but since Uncle James had chosen not to bring up the subject with Andy, Andy would respect his wishes and not discuss it either.

Andy led Uncle James's horse to the barn, unsaddled him, and filled a feed trough with oats. Then Andy showed his uncle around the farm. It was difficult for Andy to realize how much work he had done, since it had been accomplished in short periods over the months in which he had been recuperating, but Andy could tell from the look in his uncle's eyes that keeping the promise to his mother was exactly what he should have done.

"I hope you'll continue to live here at the farm,

Andy," Uncle James said. "We'll be needing all the extra hands we can find to make it productive again."

Andy said he would, but in truth, at that moment he wasn't sure what he wanted to do with his life.

Two days later Uncle Robert returned. He had George and Jimmy with him.

Andrew decided not to question them about his mother's last days, but it didn't matter because his cousins, for the most part, avoided contact with him. Everyone seemed to want to avoid talking about the war and who had died because of it.

Unlike Uncle James, Uncle Robert had only his land left. The British had burned his home and destroyed all of his belongings. Eventually he would rebuild, but for now, he and his family would be living in Uncle James's house. In many ways it was just like it had been when Andy was small, an extended family all under one roof, but Andy never could feel quite as happy as he once had.

Andy started to get restless. Schools had reopened, and he even thought about returning to the academy, since an education was another one of the things his mother had wanted so much for him. But there was still a lot of work to be done on the farm, and Andy felt a certain obligation to his uncle James to help him with it.

Andy wasn't the only one having a hard time adjusting to civilian life again. It was hard for everyone.

The people in the Waxhaws, like the patriots all over the country, had lost almost everything and were having to start their lives over. Most of the houses had either been damaged or burned to the ground. Few families had been as fortunate as Uncle James to have a nephew like Andy around to take care of their property.

One morning several weeks later, Andy was with Uncle James and Uncle Robert, trying to decide how best to repair the barn loft, when a neighbor rode up.

After they all had exchanged greetings, the neighbor said, "I hear if you make out an account of what you had taken from you by the British, the state of South Carolina will pay you for it."

"That's good news," Uncle James agreed.

"Then you and Robert here should get started

calculating your losses," the neighbor said. "I'm almost finished with mine."

After the neighbor left, Andy helped his uncles fell a couple of trees so they'd have enough lumber to repair the damaged loft in the barn, then he went about working on that while Uncle James and Uncle Robert began figuring their losses.

While he worked steadily so as not to tire himself out quickly, Andy listened to his uncles talking.

"If every man in South Carolina turns in a claim for what he's really owed," Uncle Robert said, "then there won't be enough money to go around."

Uncle James nodded his agreement. "I think what we should do is turn in a modest claim that will cover the bare necessities," he said, "and then just try to rebuild from there."

Andy's heart swelled with pride at the unselfishness of his uncles.

But as it turned out, the state treasurer thought that even their modest claims were too high and cut them almost in half.

When Uncle James learned about that, his only reaction was to shrug and say, "The state has almost no money, so this is better than nothing."

But other residents of the Carolinas weren't so generous in their reactions. Many of them packed up and moved west, to the other side of the mountains.

Andy knew they would face all kinds of hardships, including hostile Indians, just as he and Robbie had when they were with Uncle Robert's men looking for the British.

All of the talk about what people had lost because of the war opened up old wounds for Andy. He began to feel himself slipping into a dark depression again. He had lost no money, because he didn't have any to begin with, but he had lost things that couldn't be replaced. His mother and two brothers were dead. When he thought about it, his father had died for the same desire: to have his family live in a land where all men were equal under the law.

As Andy continued to do what he could to help Uncle James and Uncle Robert on the farm, he finally had to accept the fact that he would never again be as healthy as he once was.

"I have no strength after a couple of hours," he

told Uncle James, "and if I don't sit for a while in the shade, then I start to feel dizzy."

"Then that's what you should do, Andy," Uncle James said. "I know you're not shirking when you do that."

It was one thing for his uncle James to say that, and Andy believed him, but it was another thing for Andy to accept the fact that he might never again be a robust man, and to Andy, strength of character and strength of body were the most important characteristics a real man could possess.

Andy avoided looking at himself in a mirror as much as he possibly could. The scars from the British officer's sword and from the pox caused him to become filled with such anger and hatred that he was paralyzed emotionally for days at a time. When that happened, he was useless on the farm. Even the smallest of tasks was impossible for him to complete.

One afternoon when Andy was resting in the shade of one of the large trees behind the barn, Uncle Robert joined him.

"Sometimes change is good for a person, Andy,

so your uncle James and I have apprenticed you to a saddler we know, Benjamin White," he said. "He has a good leather business now and is in need of a helper."

Andy felt a tinge of anger at what his uncles had done without first talking to him about it, but he realized that he was too tired at the moment to do more than give Uncle Robert a tacit nod of agreement.

Later Andy realized that it might be a good idea to get away, to learn a new trade. "After all," he told everyone, "I love horses, and horses need saddles. I might as well learn to make good ones."

Benjamin White was the son of Joseph White, who was the uncle of Jenny Crawford, Cousin Edward's wife, so living with the White family was almost the same as living with his blood relatives. But even though the White family took Andy in as one of their own, making him feel comfortable and even loved, there was still something missing. Andy couldn't exactly put his finger on it, but he was never able to fill the void.

Andy loved horses, and he loved the smell of

leather. He became quite adept at tooling intricate designs that pleased the men who came to Benjamin White for new saddles. One of the things Andy enjoyed most was saddling up the horses with the saddles he had made, to make sure they fit perfectly, then riding the horses around the countryside. Andy had become an accomplished rider.

The work in the saddlery, while demanding, wasn't as demanding as farm labor, but after six months Andy announced, much to the dismay of Benjamin White and his family, that he was leaving to return to Uncle James's farm.

"If I'm going to sit all day, Uncle James," he said, "I might as well be sitting in school."

Two days later, after he had settled back into his old room at the farmhouse and had reestablished a comfortable routine, he packed his belongings and rode over to see Dr. Humphries.

"Do you have a place for me?" he asked Dr. Humphries.

"Well, Andrew Jackson," Dr. Humphries exclaimed, "I most certainly do have a place for you."

189

But when Andy took a seat, he realized that the rest of the boys in the class were much younger than he was, and he felt so out of place that Dr. Humphries made special arrangements for him to sit in the study to do his work. The study was where Dr. Humphries kept all of his maps. Andy returned to studying them, sometimes for hours on end, and often at the expense of what Dr. Humphries had asked him to read. Yet Dr. Humphries didn't complain. There was a strong bond and a large measure of understanding between the two.

Still, a couple of weeks later, Andy left the academy without even saying good-bye to Dr. Humphries.

Over the next few weeks Andy attended several of the newer schools that had sprung up in the Waxhaws after the end of the fighting, but he didn't like any of them.

His uncles were worried about him.

Andy sometimes stayed in his room for hours at a time, avoiding any chores, often not even coming to the table for meals, preferring instead to eat leftovers when everyone was busy somewhere else.

190

One evening, instead of eating supper with the family, Andy decided to make a complete circumference of the farm. When he returned, Uncle James was waiting for him on the front porch.

"We need to talk, Andy," Uncle James said.

Andy sat on the steps. "Yes, sir?" he said.

"We've all been through several lifetimes, what with the war and all the dying, Andy," he said, "but there comes a time when a man has to refocus his energy and to get on with his life."

"I know that, sir," Andy replied.

"Your Uncle Robert and I are worried about you," Uncle James continued. "You've started drifting through the days, not eating, not accomplishing anything to speak of."

"Well, I was thinking I might go on up to Twelve Mile Creek and farm the land that my father left us," Andy replied without hesitation. "It's been lying fallow for many years, and while I know it'll be a struggle to clear it, sir, it's rich land and will make me a living."

"Andy, one man alone can't make a go of that land," Uncle James said. "It's too wild."

Andy shrugged. "Well, sir, a person just never knows what he can do until he tries it," he said. He stood up. "Good night, sir."

Andy went inside and climbed the stairs to his room. How could he tell his uncle James that he was only searching for a way to rekindle the spirit within him?

Andy Squanders His Inheritance

Andy tried farming the land his father had left him up near Twelve Mile Creek, but his uncle had been right. It was too much for a fifteen-year-old boy who was still weakened from a stay in a British prison and hadn't yet fully recovered from a severe case of the pox.

After he left Twelve Mile Creek, Andy simply wandered around the Waxhaws, staying with first one cousin and then another, doing odd jobs in order to earn his keep. He didn't seem bothered by the fact that his life had no direction, but his relatives were getting quite concerned about him.

Andy just happened to be staying with his uncle

Robert and his family in the new farmhouse they had just finished building, when a letter for him came from northern Ireland.

A letter from overseas was quite an event in the Waxhaws, especially one from the north of Ireland, where many of the residents hated the British almost as much as the new Americans did. This letter especially attracted everyone's attention because it had a wax seal on it, letting people know—and within just a few hours, everyone did know—that this particular letter was from a very important person.

As it turned out, the letter was from a solicitor's office in Belfast, and it contained the last will and testament of Hugh Jackson, Andy's paternal grandfather.

"Grandfather Jackson is dead!" Andy exclaimed, after he had scanned the contents of the letter. "He's left me and Mother and Hugh and Robbie three hundred dollars!"

The crowd of friends and relatives who had gathered around him remained silent.

Andy looked up at them and suddenly realized

what he had said. "Of course, since they're all dead," he added sadly, "I guess that means the money is all mine."

"That it does, Andy," Uncle James said. "You've got an inheritance."

All of a sudden everyone seemed to have an opinion as to how Andy should spend his money.

"I'd take half of it and go to college to study law, Andy," Uncle Robert said. "You're a smart young man, if you'd just apply yourself."

Uncle James was shaking his head. "He can buy livestock and set up farming with that kind of money. Soon he'd be one of the wealthiest farmers in South Carolina."

Andy listened politely to all of the other suggestions, some of which he thought might be worth investigating, but he knew that he first had to get the money before he could do anything with it.

"According to this letter," Andy said, "I have to go to the law offices of Littlefield and Smythe in Charles Town to pick up the money."

"You can take that mare of mine that you just

shod, Andy," Uncle Robert said. "She'll get you there and back safely."

That set off another flurry of discussion, with his cousins and their friends talking about what clothes Andy should take with him. They all soon realized that Andy hadn't exactly been keeping his clothes in the best of shape, so water was fetched and the big black kettles were filled and fires were started underneath them.

For the next couple of hours, every woman there helped to wash, dry, and iron Andy's clothes, then pack them neatly in saddle bags.

Andy was amazed at all of the sudden attention he was now getting. Of course, he thought he understood what had happened. He was no longer a problem relative, someone drifting from house to house. While he hadn't exactly been begging for food, he was certainly putting himself in a position where his relatives felt obligated to offer it to him, plus a bed to sleep in. More than once Andy had the distinct feeling that they had begun to dread his arrival. Now they didn't seem to be able to do enough for him.

Finally, with his saddlebags full of food and clothing and with his head full of advice, Andy was ready to leave for Charles Town. He mounted the mare and headed toward the road in front of Uncle Robert's house.

For the first time since his mother's death, Andy thought he detected a spark of happiness somewhere deep inside him. He was on his way to Charles Town. Soon, he knew, his pockets would be bulging with his grandfather's money.

Andy rode until it got dark, stopping overnight in the meadow, where—it seemed so long ago—they had stopped on the cattle drive to Charles Town. His mother and his brothers had still been alive then.

By the light of the campfire Andy reread the letter from Ireland several times. When he awakened the next morning, he read the letter again.

"It is true!" he said. "It's not a dream!"

Andy fed his horse, then ate some of the food his relatives and their friends had packed for him, reread the letter, and then mounted his horse to continue the trip to Charles Town.

While he rode he mulled over all of the advice he had been given. Some of it was very good advice, Andy knew, and some of it wasn't, but it really didn't matter at this point in his life, he decided. He now had money, plenty of it, it seemed, and he didn't have to answer to anyone as to how he spent it.

But how should he spend the money? he wondered.

Studying law, which was Uncle Robert's idea, began to intrigue him.

Andy had heard that before the war most of the lawyers in the Carolinas were Tories, but now they had been disbarred from the courts. He knew what that meant. There would be a great need for lawyers who had been loyal to the Congress.

The more Andy thought about it, the more it made sense to him. Andrew Jackson, lawyer! He really liked the sound of that.

Late the next day, Andy came to a road sign that said: CHARLESTON, 15 MILES.

Andy blinked his eyes, closed them, then looked at the sign again. It still said: CHARLESTON, 15 MILES

Something wasn't right here. Was he on the wrong road? he wondered. He looked around. Of course, it had been several years since the cattle drive, but there were still quite a few landmarks that Andy remembered. So what had happened to *Charles Town*?

Just then he saw the dust of an approaching traveler headed north. When the rider had almost reached him, Andy began waving his arms, signaling the rider to stop.

"Is there a problem I can help you with, young man?" the rider asked.

Andy didn't think the rider seemed much older than he was, but there was something about him that made Andy feel inferior.

"Yes, sir," Andy said. He pointed to the sign. "I was heading to Charles Town, but now I think I'm on the wrong road."

The young man gave him a hearty laugh. "You're not on the wrong road at all," he said. "Charles Town has been renamed Charleston."

"Why?" Andy asked.

"Well, that should be plain enough to most

patriots," the young man said, rather haughtily, Andy thought. "The new name sounds less like the town belongs to some British king!"

Andy had to agree that that made a lot of sense, but he wished this stranger weren't acting so high and mighty about everything.

"Well, it might take me a while to get used to calling it Charleston instead of Charles Town," Andy said, "but I'm certainly going to make the effort."

"Oh? Are you planning to stay in Charleston for a while?" the young man asked him. He gave Andy the once over. "How old are you, anyway?"

"I'm fifteen, so I can do what I want to do!" Andy said. Against his better judgment, he added, "I've inherited a lot of money. I have to go to a lawyer's office to pick it up."

The main raised an eyebrow. "Well, that just might make a difference, if you'll use your money to buy some new clothes," he said. "If you plan to mix with the right people, then you'll need to dress like they do."

"Do the right people stay at the Quarter Horse Tavern?" Andy asked. "That's where we stayed when

I went on a cattle drive, and that's where I thought I'd stay this time."

The man shrugged. "It's all right, but I don't think you'll meet any of the *best* people there," he said. He sniffed. "Of course, dressed as you are now, some of the better inns might make you feel uncomfortable."

Andy and the young man, who finally said his name was Jonathan Scaffold, talked for a few more minutes, with Scaffold saying that when he got back from Charlotte, perhaps he would look Andy up at the Quarter Horse Tavern and introduce him to his friends.

When Andy resumed his journey, he knew he had passed another milestone in his life. Now he felt as though he wasn't even going to the same town, and after the conversation with Jonathan Scaffold—even if Scaffold never did look him up in Charleston—he thought he better understood how important money was to a person. It could buy you goods, such as cattle and clothes, but it could also buy you friendships. It hadn't been lost on Andy how Jonathan Scaffold's opinion of him had changed when he mentioned his inheritance.

Andy wondered if that should have made him angry. He knew it hadn't. He merely saw it as the way people with money acted toward other people with money. Scaffold hadn't known that Andy had money when they met on the road, but once he found out, Scaffold realized that they had something in common after all.

Suddenly Andy was surprised at how well he could remember things from his first trip to Charleston, especially the elegantly dressed women and the men in their satin coats and breeches. He knew he could feel at home with these people, now that he had money himself.

Andy reached Charleston at noon and rode immediately to the Quarter Horse Tavern. At first he thought he was in the wrong place, because for some reason the tavern didn't seem as grand has it had when they stayed there on the cattle drive. Jonathan Scaffold had been right. This probably wasn't a place that the best people in Charleston would stay. Still, it was a place he was familiar with, and he could think about staying somewhere else tomorrow—or perhaps the day after tomorrow. There were too many other important things to do in Charleston to worry about that now, he finally decided, such as paying a visit to the lawyer's office to get the money that Grandfather Jackson had left him.

Andy washed up in a basin that was on a stand next to his bed, combed his hair, and then put on what he thought was probably his newest shirt, although when he looked at himself in a mirror, he saw only a poor country boy in a misshapen piece of homespun cloth.

As Andy headed for the lawyer's office, he began to make a list of the things he was going to do to change himself.

"Ah, Mr. Jackson! I've been expecting you," the lawyer said, introducing himself as the Smythe of Littlefield and Smythe. "I trust your trip down to Charleston was uneventful."

"Yes, sir," Andy said, "I had no problems whatsoever."

"It's wonderful that things are back to normal, now that the war is over," Smythe said. "Well, I should say that things are almost back to normal, as I do understand that things in your part of South Carolina are still, shall we say, rather difficult."

Andy allowed as how they were, but hastened to add that the people of the Waxhaws were tough and that everyone would soon be back on their feet again.

With the pleasantries out of the way, Mr. Smythe and his assistant produced papers for Andy to sign, which he did with a flourish, and in less than an hour, the last part of which was devoted to Mr. Smythe's giving Andy the name of his tailor and advice on what wealthy men in Charleston were wearing this fashion season, Andy left the offices of Littlefield and Smythe with the sum of three hundred dollars in his pockets.

Andy walked directly to Oliver & Sons, Tailors, which was across the street from the law office.

There Mr. Jackson, as Mr. Oliver called him, was measured for three suits.

"I'd like to have the suits tomorrow morning," Andy told him.

Without hesitating, Mr. Oliver said, "Of course,

sir, although there will be an extra charge for that, as I shall have to bring in two more tailors to help me, but they are some of the best tailors in the city of Charleston, and you will not be disappointed in their work."

"Naturally," Andy said. He paid Mr. Oliver the extra amount without a quibble.

When Andy left the tailor's, he stopped at the Gold Lion Inn and ate rare roast beef and potatoes. It was one of the best meals he had had in quite some time. What was beginning to amaze Andy the most was how quickly the war seemed to have disappeared from Charleston. It was almost as though it had never happened.

This impression was furthered after Andy left the inn and walked along Board Path to the military wall to look at the fort. Along the way he saw people building fences and repairing buildings and houses. Yes, he decided, things move faster in Charleston than they do in the Waxhaws.

That night Andy had a difficult time sleeping at the Quarter Horse Tavern. Revelers kept him awake with their loud singing and arguments, but he wasn't sure he could have slept even if it had been totally quiet. His mind was racing with all the things he wanted to do while he was in Charleston.

Right before dawn he did doze off, but a nearby rooster got him up shortly afterward, and he quickly dressed, ate a breakfast of some of the food from his saddlebags, and then headed for the tailor's.

As promised, his suits were ready, and the two extra tailors Mr. Oliver had hired to help him stood by smiling as Andy tried on each of the three suits.

The coats and the breeches fit him exceedingly well, as he would have expected, but his boots were dirty, scarred, and certainly marked him as being from the country.

"Well, we can take care of that," Mr. Oliver said. "One street over, behind this establishment, actually, is the best cobbler in Charleston, Samuel Stone."

There was a chorus of agreement from the other tailors.

"Then I shall go there next," Andy told them. With that, he picked up his suits, neatly folded, and headed out to see Samuel Stone.

Of course, once Andy had his new boots, he

realized that he was still not finished with his appearance. He now needed a haircut and a hat.

"Could you suggest a hatter and a barber?" he asked the cobbler.

"Of course," the cobbler said.

Two hours later Andy returned to the Quarter Horse Tavern. When he was fully dressed in one of his new suits, his new boots, and his new hat, he didn't recognize himself. He no longer looked like Andy Jackson of the Waxhaws, he looked like Andrew Jackson, citizen of Charleston.

When other men and women saw Andy strolling down Broad Path, they nodded. Some of them, from time to time, even stopped to talk, and it wasn't long before Andy had made quite a few friends. These friends in turn introduced him to other friends.

"We're going to the races this afternoon, Jackson," some new friends said. "Why don't you come along?"

Andy gladly accompanied them. When they bet on a particular horse, he bet more.

"There's a cockfight tonight, Jackson," other new

friends said. "If you've never been to one, then you've never been to Charleston."

"Oh, I've been to them before," Andy said, "and I promised myself that I would go back."

So, for the next two weeks Andy went to every fight in the city, always betting on the cocks that his new friends suggested, because that seemed to be what he was expected to do.

"Sorry, Jackson," his new friends would say when the cock he bet on was killed. "Better luck next time."

Andy shrugged it off. After all, he told them, it was only money, and if there was one thing Andy knew, it was that he had plenty of money.

Occasionally one of his new friends, usually a woman, would ask him what he planned to do with his life.

Andy would shrug. "Why can't this be my life? Why is it that I have to do anything else?" he would say flippantly. He would wave his arms around, pointing to whatever it was they were doing at the time. "I'm perfectly content as it is."

Then one morning Andy's money was gone.

He had awakened, as usual, planning to meet two new friends at another inn for breakfast, when he realized that he had no money in his pockets. If he went to the races or if he went to the cockfights, he would have to have money, because if his new friends bet, then he would have to bet too. Spending lots of money seemed to be one of the requirements for being accepted among the best people of Charleston.

"Maybe I put the rest of the money in the pockets of my other coats," Andy said.

He hurried over to the armoire and searched through the pockets of his coats and pants several times, but he didn't find so much as one coin.

Next he made a mad dash to the stables where his horse was quartered and frantically searched through his saddlebags, but he found only some moldy pieces of food he hadn't removed since he had taken to eating in the finest inns in Charleston.

As Andy made his way back through the inn, the innkeeper, a Mr. Dundee, stopped him with, "I hate to bother you with this, Mr. Jackson, but if you'll remember, when you arrived, I told you that your bill must be settled each week, and you've yet to settle it for three weeks."

Andy blinked. Vaguely he remembered telling the man that he would settle the bill when he got back from the races or from a cockfight or from a particular party with some of his new friends.

"Have I honestly not done that?" Andy asked. He was totally confounded.

The innkeeper shook his head. "No, sir, you haven't." He handed Andy a piece of paper.

Andy looked at it. He owed the inn thirty dollars. How was he going to pay this bill, he wondered, when he didn't have a cent to his name?

He took a deep breath and faced the innkeeper. "I assure you that I shall take care of this bill by the end of the day," he said. "First I need to talk to my lawyer. He handles all of my money."

"Of course, Mr. Jackson," the innkeeper said. "That is quite satisfactory." He nodded at Andy and headed back toward the kitchen.

Andy returned to the stable. He had to think, and he always thought better when he was on his horse. He had to figure out a way to come up with thirty dollars. If he rode around Charleston for a few hours, he decided, then maybe he could think of a way to make some money.

Andy saddled his horse, mounted her, and started out the stable door opposite the inn. He had to ride by a group of stable hands who were involved in a dice game.

"You've got the best-looking horse of anyone at the inn," one of the men said to him. "I'd give almost anything to have a horse like that."

Andy reined in. He had suddenly thought of a solution to his problem. "What's your name?" he asked.

"Jones," the man replied.

"Well, Jones, would you give me thirty dollars for this horse?" Andy said.

"Thirty dollars, sir?" Jones exclaimed.

"You heard me," Andy replied.

Quickly Jones huddled with the other players. After a couple of minutes they pushed all their money into one pile.

"You're on," Jones said.

Andy handed the reins of his horse to one of the

men standing closest to him and squatted down in front of Jones. The man handed him the dice. Andy shook them, never taking his eyes off Jones. Suddenly he stopped shaking the dice, stood up, and said, "I'd like another pair of dice. I don't like the feel of these."

Jones started to argue, but Andy stepped forward, towering over the man, so Jones quickly scooped up another pair of dice and handed them to Andy.

Andy shook these, then grinned, and said, "Much better, Mr. Jones."

Quickly he threw the dice.

The men gasped. Jones's eyes seem to go blank.

"I won!" Andy said, not quite believing it himself. "I won!"

He scooped up all the money in the pile, then mounted his horse, and rode her back into the stable, where he unsaddled her and put her back in the stall.

Andy counted the money he had won. It totaled forty dollars.

All of a sudden Andy broke out in a cold sweat. He felt as if he had just awakened from a nightmare.

He had spent his entire inheritance, and on what? Horse races. Cockfights. Fancy clothes. The best food. Now he had no money to use for any of the things his relatives had suggested to him or that he himself had thought about using it for. "I am such a fool!" Andy said.

He turned to look at his horse. "And I almost lost you on a roll of the dice," he said as he nuzzled the horse's soft nose. "You don't even belong to me. You really belong to Uncle Robert. He still needs more horses to help him at the farm, but he was willing to let me take you to Charleston because I'm family, and I needed a way here so I could pick up my inheritance."

The thought of everything that he had done was making Andy sick to his stomach. How was he going to face his relatives? he wondered. "How could I have been so stupid?" Andy demanded of himself.

Andy left the horse and headed to find the innkeeper. He paid his bill, then he went to his room, packed his belongings, and headed back toward the Waxhaws.

He tried not to think about what his uncles would say to him when he told them he had squandered all of his inheritance.

"I will never again throw the dice," Andy promised himself as he rode north. "I have proved myself to be a fool, but on this I will keep my word!"

Frontier Lawyer

"You did *what?*" Uncle James demanded.

Andy reluctantly repeated to his uncles and his other relatives the story of how he had squandered all of his inheritance in Charleston.

"Andrew Jackson, your mother is probably turning over in her grave," Uncle James said. There were tears in his eyes. "Do you know how this makes me feel, son? Do you? I promised your mother I would always take care of you, and now you've gone and ruined your future."

Andy swallowed hard. He felt absolutely miserable. When he thought about what had happened in Charleston, it was as if it had happened to somebody else. Now that he was back in the Waxhaws, sitting in a hard chair, listening to everyone rant and rave about how incredibly selfish and stupid he had been, he began to feel as if they were actually talking about somebody else, certainly not about him. How could Andrew Jackson do something like that?

This went on for several weeks, until one day Andy decided that he was tired of listening to all of them repeat themselves, so he packed his things and simply rode away without telling anyone where he was going or what he was going to do.

Actually, Andy himself didn't know what he would do. Once again he began drifting through life. Fortunately the drifting lasted only a couple of weeks, during which time he often spent the night camped out close to the home of a relative. At first he wondered why he would ride all over the Waxhaws during the day, stopping only to feed and water himself and his horse, then return to a meadow or an isolated barn on land belonging to family.

Finally, one morning when he awakened, he knew *that* day would be different. Andy had heard of a school run by Robert McCulloch over in York County, just a few miles south of Charlotte. Andy returned to school. He wasn't so much interested in sitting in a classroom again as he was in finding out just how much more McCulloch knew than he did.

As it turned out, it wasn't much, although Andy made sure that he was never disrespectful in class. Andy soon approached McCulloch to talk to him about what had precipitated his coming back to school.

"I admire what you do, sir," Andy told McCulloch. "I have, in fact, thought it might be my calling."

"Well, I'm a bit surprised, Mr. Jackson, as I thought that a career in education might be toward the bottom of what you had planned to do with your life," McCulloch said. "But as for knowledge, yes, I should say that you most certainly are quite prepared to impart various courses of study to the young men of South Carolina."

With that recommendation ringing in his ears, along with a letter from Robert McCulloch stating the same, Andy rode all over the northern part of South Carolina in search of teaching jobs.

His commanding presence, his way with words, and the recommendation from McCulloch, who was a very respected educator in the Carolinas, were enough to get him hired at an academy similar to the one run by Dr. Humphries. But he quickly realized that this was not the lifelong career for him.

"Is there a problem, Mr. Jackson?" the headmaster, Charles Richardson, asked him one evening at dinner. "You've not said much of anything all evening."

"No, sir, no problem," Andy replied. "I was just thinking about what I want to do with my life."

"Hmm. I gather that since our initial meeting, where you said you thought educating the young men of South Carolina was your calling, you've changed your mind," Richardson said.

Andy nodded. "Yes, sir, I have," he replied, "although please understand, I will not be leaving anytime soon. After all, I gave you my word that I would stay here at least a year, and my word is as good as gold."

"I have no doubt of that, Mr. Jackson. I believe

myself to be a good judge of men," Richardson said. "I am, however, always interested in helping young men find their true calling. Please keep in mind that my library is always open to you. I do have books on many different subjects, one of which might be just the spark you need to help you see what God has already ordained for you."

"Thank you, sir," Andy said, promising to take full advantage of Richardson's library, but at the moment not wanting to listen to one of Richardson's sermons, which he was fond of giving at the drop of a hat.

Andy excused himself and headed for his room.

Andy more than kept his promise to Richardson and stayed at the academy for almost two years, becoming one of the favorite instructors of the boys who went there. During that time, with the help of certain books in Richardson's library, Andy thought he had finally decided what he wanted to do with his life.

While he was at Richardson's academy, Andy had no contact whatsoever with his family, and after he decided to leave, he told no one except

Richardson. Andy actually couldn't even explain this himself, but he no longer felt any emotional attachment to his relatives and would never again return to the Waxhaws.

In 1784, the first full year of peace following the Revolutionary War, Andy set his sights on Salisbury, North Carolina, which was about forty miles northwest of Charlotte. At that time Salisbury was an important town in a part of the state know as the Back Country.

Andy had finally decided to pursue law as a career. In order to do that, he had to apprentice himself to a well-known lawyer. Andy's only regret was that he hadn't decided this earlier. He often remembered how, on the road to Charleston to collect his inheritance, he had definitely been considering law as a career. Unfortunately, squandering his entire inheritance had left him not only without the money to pursue this calling, but also with the feeling that, as a human being who had weaknesses for horse racing and cockfighting, he simply wasn't worthy of anything so lofty.

When Andy arrived in Salisbury, he went immediately to see Spruce McCay, an eminent lawyer in the Carolinas.

"I have decided to become a lawyer just like you," Andy announced to McCay.

At first McCay thought this tall, red-headed boy standing in front of him was simply some country bumpkin who had fallen on his head once too often, but the more McCay listened to him, the more impressed he was.

"I've been teaching for almost two years, down in York County, South Carolina, at Mr. Richardson's academy," Andy said. He handed McCay the letter of recommendation that Richardson had written for him. "I've saved my money, and I can pay you well."

"How old are you, son?" McCay asked.

"I'm eighteen, sir," Andy replied, "or just three months shy of it, anyway."

"Well, Andrew Jackson, I'd be pleased to teach you what law I know," McCay said. "I'm a pretty good judge of character myself, and I have a feeling that you're going to go far in this young country of ours."

"I have that feeling too, sir," Andy replied honestly.

For the first time in many years, Andy was pleased with himself, but at the back of his mind was always the nagging feeling that he would bungle this opportunity too. As things seemed to get better and better for him, he began to relax. He had come to Salisbury without any urging from his relatives, having made his own decision, and he had been accepted on his own merit. Slowly the feeling of inadequacy that had plagued him almost all his life began to disappear.

Eventually Andy began to feel at home in Salisbury. He certainly liked it much better than living on a farm in the Waxhaws. Although Salisbury could not be called a city, like Charleston or Charlotte, it had wide shaded streets that allowed people to stroll comfortably, even during the heat of a summer day. There were some houses that looked like the ones he had seen in Charleston. Of course, there were also a lot of log cabins, but even those were surrounded by beautiful and well-tended gardens. Frankly Andy was glad that Salisbury didn't have cockfighting or horse racing. That way, he told himself, he would never be tempted.

"Well, Salisbury likes you too, Andy," Mrs. McCay told him one evening, when Andy mentioned how well he had been treated. With a twinkle in her eye, she added, "After all, you're tall, slender, and quite intelligent."

Andy grinned. "Well, thank you, ma'am," he said. "I must say that I have been charmed by all of the ladies of Salisbury since I've been here."

"So I hear," Mrs. McCay teased him.

This remark puzzled Andy somewhat, as he had never thought of himself as being particularly attractive to the opposite sex.

Late one evening Andy and John NcNairy, one of Andy's best friends and another one of Mr. McCay's law students, were sitting on the front porch of the Rowan House, where they both boarded, Andy asked John to explain why he thought all of the women fawned over him.

"You're an easy talker, glib, and you have a quick smile," John said.

"I also have a long face, scarred by the pox and the sword of a British officer," Andy countered.

"But girls find that intriguing, Andy," John said. He held up his hands to stave off further discussion. "Please don't ask me to explain the female mind!"

"Oh, heaven forbid that I should do that," Andy said.

"Further, Mr. Jackson, if you add to that how the men of Salisbury have accepted you, not only as one of them but as one of their leaders," John said, "then I'd say you are probably the most roundly respected man in town."

Andy felt genuinely touched by his friend's comments. He vowed silently to continue to make sure the people of Salisbury felt that way. Especially since, from time to time, he still had lingering doubts about his character, as though this were all a dream from which he could suddenly be awakened, only to find himself back in the Waxhaws, behind in his chores again.

Andy enjoyed living at the Rowan House. It was a very pleasant place to be, not only because of Mrs. Rowan, who treated all her tenants like they were her children, but also because the other men who lived there were young and ambitious and full of excitement about what the future held for America.

Andy's days were spent studying law with McNairy and another student, Stephen Buckingham, in the small house by Spruce McCay's garden that served as an office. From dawn to dusk the three of them read law books, copied long reports that McCay needed for his court cases, and ran errands for him. If McCay wasn't busy preparing to argue a case in a court in some other part of the Carolinas, he would sometimes tell them about past trials and explain to them how he defended the accused.

Studying law was very hard work, but Andy and the others really enjoyed it. After they left the house, though, they made sure that their plans for the evening included things that would take their minds off their studies.

In late 1786, Spruce McCay called Andy into his study and said, "I've been watching you, Andy, and I'm quite pleased with how you've progressed

here, but I've decided that I've taught you everything I know."

"Sir?" Andy said. He was completely taken
aback by the remark. "Does this mean that I'm
being dismissed for some cause?" He had settled
into such a comfortable routine in Salisbury that
he didn't want to give it up.

McCay shook his head. "Of course not, Andy.
You should have more faith in your abilities," he
said. "I've made arrangements for you to continue
your study of law with Colonel John Stokes, one of
the best lawyers in North Carolina."

Andy's spirits soared. Colonel John Stokes was
also one of the bravest soldiers of the Revolutionary
War and had become a friend of the Jackson family.
Stokes had lost a hand in battle and had been
nursed back to health by Andy's mother. Andy
had spent hours talking to him. When Colonel
Stokes had returned home, he had ordered a
local silversmith to fashion a silver knob to replace
his hand. Everyone in the Carolinas knew stories
about how Stokes, in court, would pound on a
table with the knob to emphasize various points

of the particular argument he was making.

Any student would jump at the chance to study with Colonel Stokes, so Andy packed his belongings, said good-bye to his friends, and headed for the Stokeses' house on the banks of the Catawba River, just west of Charlotte. He would be staying and studying there for the next six months. Any doubt that Andy might have had about leaving Salisbury was immediately dispelled by the warmth with which he was welcomed into the Stokes family. Andy knew right away that he was home.

In the summer of 1787 Andy completed his legal training under Colonel Stokes. On September 26, 1787, he appeared for examination before two judges of the Superior Court of Law and Equity of North Carolina, Samuel Ashe and John F. Williams. They described him as a man whose moral character was unblemished and who was extremely competent in his knowledge of the law and authorized him to practice as an attorney in the courts within the state.

Andrew Jackson, lawyer, was now just a few months past his twentieth birthday. He was tall, more than six feet, and he moved with the grace of a natural athlete. His hair had darkened to where it was more auburn than red, and he let it fall over his forehead, allowing it to hide some of the scars from the pox, about which he was still a little sensitive. Andy knew that he cut a striking figure, which pleased him to no end, but he was prouder of his knowledge of the law, which he felt was equal to that of any of the lawyers in any of the other states.

At that time in North Carolina, as well as in some of the other states, judges and lawyers were forced to travel from town to town because courts were only held for one week at a time, twice each year, in each location. This was called "making a circuit."

Shortly after Andy was certified, the first court was held in Salisbury, and it came two months after the Constitution of the United States had been written in Philadelphia. When Andy was younger this would have been of great interest, but now he hardly noticed it, because he was completely focused on his first day in court.

Everything went exceedingly well for Andy. The people of Salisbury seemed proud to have him among them once again. Andy had bought new clothes for his return, and eyes followed him wherever he went.

Even the judge seemed impressed. "You're an exceptionally good lawyer, Jackson," he said at the close of arguments on the second day. "You have a great future ahead of you."

"Thank you, Your Honor," Andy said.

"You ought to think about going out west," the judge continued, surprising Andy somewhat. "They need good lawyers, and someone like you could really make a name for himself in a very short period of time."

When the people of the Carolinas said "out west," they were talking about the long, oblong strip of land on the other side of the Allegheny Mountains that was known as the Western District of North Carolina. It was a wild land, and for as long as Andy could remember, inhabited only by fur traders and Indians. But with the end of the war, more and more Carolinians had been moving there to settle the fertile river valleys, most notably the Cumberland.

But the state of North Carolina was finding it difficult to govern this vast territory. So, without consulting the settlers, who thought they were still residents of the state, the governor, with the assent of the legislature, gave the land to the United States in payment of war debts.

When the settlers found out about it, they were understandably angry. If North Carolina doesn't want us anymore, then we'll make our own state, they decided, and declared the territory the state of Freeland, with John Sevier, the hero of the Battle of King's Mountain, as the governor. Unfortunately no one paid any attention to them, including the federal government. The residents changed the name to the state of Franklin and asked Benjamin Franklin to help them, but even he wasn't interested in a place so far away. Finally, three years later, North Carolina reclaimed the area.

Meanwhile Andy continued to ride the circuit, still thinking from time to time about what the judge had said regarding his going out west, but dismissing it each time, as more and more he had begun to question his new profession.

"You can hardly make a living at it," he complained. "You can't put down roots if you have to pick up and move to a different town every two days."

Andy had almost decided to quit, to stay in the next town he came to, and to find a job doing anything but practicing law, but then he met his old friend and fellow law student from Salisbury, John McNairy, who talked him out of it.

"Take a look at this paper," John said, handing Andy an official-looking document.

Andy took the paper and glanced over it. "You're a judge in the Western District!" he exclaimed. "How did that happen?"

"The governor appointed me," John said. "How about going with me to Jonesborough?"

Andy shrugged. "The governor appointed you," he said. "He didn't appoint me."

"Listen, Andy, I was in the right place at the right time," John explained. "It's not because I'm a better lawyer than anyone else, especially you."

"Well, that's the truth," Andy said with a grin.

John gave him a good-natured punch on the arm. "And I soon found out that as a judge I have the power to make appointments, and I'm appointing you public prosecutor if you want the job."

"*If* I want the job!" Andy shouted. "Well, what do you think?"

They immediately started to make plans.

The journey to Jonesborough would be over several hundred miles of rugged mountains and forested valleys, through land inhabited by Indians, and land that was unexplored, but nothing could dissuade Andy that his decision to follow John McNairy was anything but the right one.

Horses were the only means of transportation. Andy and John would take two each. They both had always selected their horses wisely and cared for them, and this time was no exception.

Andy really didn't want to leave behind the horse that had been faithful to him for these last few years, but he was afraid that the arduous journey would be too difficult for the mare, so he reluctantly traded her for a younger mare and then bought a second one.

In their saddlebags Andy and John packed their law books, clothing they thought would be suitable for the frontier, two pistols each, and enough food to last them for several days.

The journey was difficult, but their excitement at starting a new life on the frontier kept at bay any negative feelings about what they were doing.

Andy and John arrived in Jonesborough in the late summer of 1788. They found a settlement of about sixty log cabins and a log courthouse. The latter was something they had not expected, because elsewhere court was often held in someone's house.

When Andy mentioned this to one of the residents, the man said, "You'll find a lot of legal work to do here. There are plenty of cases of boundary line disputes and unpaid bills. If we met in someone's house, we'd either be changing houses every day or completely disrupting the daily life of a good man and his family."

"I can well understand that," Andy agreed. He liked the idea of a separate building in which to argue his cases. Turning to John, he added, "I think we need to stay here awhile."

John agreed with him.

Together they rented a room in a cabin belonging to a local merchant.

The people of Jonesborough liked Andy and John immediately. They thought the men eminently fair in their judgments. In fact, on many occasions Andy was able to settle arguments out of court.

Andy and John made themselves useful to the community in other ways too. When they weren't involved in legal issues, they built cabins, chopped down trees, and even, from time to time, helped some of the young ladies of Jonesborough husk ears of corn.

That fall a wagon train of about forty families came to Jonesborough on their way farther west to a settlement called French Lick. Each family had been given government land in payment for their service in the Revolutionary War. Their excitement infected both Andy and John.

Late one night Andy said, "John, you're the judge of this whole territory, but you've only seen part of it. Our work here is done, so I say that it's time for you to see the rest of it, and as your public prosecutor, I'll go with you."

John got out of bed, lit a lamp, and said, "Well, what are we waiting for, then?"

Within minutes they had packed their belongings, saddled their horses, and joined the wagon train just as it was pulling out of Jonesborough.

It was one of the most arduous journeys that Andy had ever undertaken. At night he and John were ready to collapse, hoping that they wouldn't be asked to stand watch, because they were afraid they'd fall asleep.

From time to time Andy and John would look at each other and, in unspoken language, communicate that this might not have been such a good idea after all.

For several days they saw no signs of human life, not even the Indians they had been expecting, and the settlers soon began to drop their guard. At night when the wagon train halted and the fires had been started, some of the men would hunt game in the surrounding woods, leaving the camp virtually unprotected. After the women cooked the evening meal, they would spread blankets on the

open ground and sleep heavily until first light with their children snuggled up around them.

Then one night when Andy had watch, he suddenly developed an uneasy feeling. Why he really wasn't sure, but a sixth sense told him there was going to be trouble.

All around him the camp was silent, except for the snoring of some of the men, and then suddenly, some distance away he heard the hooting of an owl.

Andy felt the hair rise on the back of his neck. Quietly he picked up his musket.

The owl hooted again, but this time it seemed to be on the other side of the camp.

Slowly Andy crawled to where John was sleeping and gently shook his shoulder. "We're surrounded by Indians," he whispered. "I'm sure of it."

John sat up and listened to the hooting sounds. "What do you think we should do?" he whispered.

"I don't think they'll attack until dawn," Andy whispered, "so I think we need to wake up everyone and, making as little noise as possible, get out of here fast."

It proved almost impossible to whisper warnings

loud enough to make the sleepy settlers understand the seriousness of the situation, but they finally managed. About an hour before dawn the wagon train pulled out of the camp, leaving roaring fires to fool their attackers, but taking people who continued to grumble about the invisible Indians.

Several days later a lone rider overtook them and reported a massacre of settlers who had camped in the same spot. After that, the grumbling stopped. Now Andy and John were their heroes.

Finally, as the maples began to turn scarlet, the wagon train arrived at French Lick only to learn that the settlement on the Cumberland River had been renamed Nashborough in honor of a war hero. The residents of Nashborough, which one day would be renamed Nashville, welcomed the newcomers with open arms. They wanted more and more people, not only to help them settle this beautiful territory but for additional protection against Indian attacks.

The residents were especially glad to have Andrew Jackson and John McNairy.

"We need more folks like you to help bring

justice to this place," one of the residents told them.

A man came up to Andy, held out his hand, and said, "I'm John Overton from Kentucky. Do you and Judge McNairy have a place to stay?"

"No, as a matter of fact, we don't," Andy told him. "Can you recommend one?"

"I'm very happy with my quarters at the Widow Donelson's home. She and her daughter Rachel have taken in several boarders," Overton said. "They're actually living in the blockhouse, just a few steps away from the main cabin where the rest of us live. If you like, I can put in a good word for the both of you."

Andy saw that John was busy giving legal advice to a crowd of townspeople, so instead of interrupting him, he said, "We'd like that very much."

"Well, then, when you and Judge McNairy are ready, we'll ride out there," Overton said. "I think you'll be very happy there." He paused and then added, "And in Nashborough, too."

"Oh, there's no doubt about that," Andy said. "I already am."

Andrew and Rachel

In Nashville Andrew Jackson prospered. He bought land and he bought slaves. He also fell in love with his landlady's daughter, Rachel, who at the time was married to a Captain Lewis Robards. Robards was ill-bred and had a violent temper. Rachel told Andrew that she had come back to live with her mother because she realized that she was not in love with her husband and had even begun to fear for her life. From that moment on, Andrew devoted his life to protecting Rachel.

In 1791, when Andrew received the news that the Virginia legislature had granted Robards a divorce from Rachel, he proposed to her, and they were married a few days later. Unfortunately the news of the divorce proved false.

In 1794, Andrew learned that Robards had not gotten the divorce until 1793, which meant that Andrew's marriage to Rachel was not legal. They were stunned by the news and immediately remarried.

Later, political enemies of Andrew Jackson would charge him with having stolen another man's wife. When this happened, though, Jackson's temper would turn violent. Any man who made such a remark about Rachel often became the victim of a horsewhip or a dueling pistol.

One such victim was another Nashville lawyer, Charles Dickinson, whom Andrew shot in a duel, because Dickinson had made disparaging remarks about Rachel.

Such actions helped build Andrew Jackson's reputation for being a man of iron will and determination, but it also allowed his enemies to point to such deeds as examples of how Jackson took pleasure in brutality and violence.

What had been the Western District of North Carolina eventually became the state of Tennessee, and in 1796, Andrew Jackson won election as its first representative to Congress. In Washington, Jackson's strong anti-British feelings—the result of all he and his family had suffered during the American Revolution—put him in opposition to most of the other politicians in Washington. This also created political problems for him back in Tennessee.

Jackson eventually aligned himself with William Blount, a Tennessee senator, in order to stave off an attempt to unseat him. Behind this attempt was the governor of Tennessee, John Sevier of the Battle of King's Mountain fame. In 1797, Jackson was elected to the United States Senate, but financial difficulties forced him to resign that post in 1798.

Back home in Tennessee, Jackson was appointed to the Superior Court of Tennessee, which not only helped his financial situation but also brought him respect because of his legal opinions. "Do what is *right* between parties," he told the members of the court. "That is what the law always *means*."

This was a very pleasant period in Andrew and Rachel's life. In 1802, Andrew became a major general in the Tennessee militia. After he retired from the court in 1804, Jackson dedicated himself to building his new home, which he called the Hermitage. It was a few miles northeast of Nashville. There, he also started raising thoroughbred horses, which helped him forget the uncertainties of growing cotton.

In 1805 one of Jackson's guests at the Hermitage was Aaron Burr, vice president under President Thomas Jefferson. Like so many others at the time, Jackson thought that Burr was interested only in forcing Spain to give up Mexico and that he had the best interests of the United States at heart. Jackson agreed to help Burr build some boats. Shortly after this agreement, however, Jackson decided that perhaps Burr's interest in Mexico was self-serving. He cut off all contact with Burr. In later years, though, Jackson came to believe that Aaron Burr was a misunderstood

patriot whose political career had been sabotaged by Thomas Jefferson.

This idyllic period in the lives of Andrew and Rachel Jackson lasted until 1812.

Fighting the British—Again!

Andrew Jackson was glad the United States declared war on Britain in 1812 over shipping and territory disputes.

Earlier Jackson had criticized the government's submissions to Britain, calling Presidents Thomas Jefferson and James Madison cowards. Now Jackson eagerly offered his military expertise for the invasions of Canada and Florida, even though it would mean a long separation from his beloved Rachel, who would remain at the Hermitage in Nashville. Unfortunately Jackson's past undiplomatic comments about how the administrations in Washington were ruining the country hadn't endeared him to what was referred to as the "Virginia Dynasty." Because of that, Jackson had to settle for a commission as major general of United States Volunteers. He was ordered to lead his men to Natchez, Mississippi, to support the forces of General James Wilkinson. But after several months during which Jackson and his men never saw any sign of the enemy, the government decided his command was useless and had it disbanded.

Jackson's political foes in Washington now hoped that he would seem like a ridiculous figure, but they had unwittingly given him even more fame. On the grueling march back to Tennessee, Jackson was so tough and efficient that he became known forever as "Old Hickory." Once again Jackson had won a battle without actually facing his enemy.

In 1813, Jackson was again called back to military duty. The Creek Indians had massacred settlers at Fort Mims, in what was then Mississippi Territory. Even though Jackson didn't have sufficient supplies and was hampered by men who were more interested in mutinying than in fighting Indians, he was able to crush the Creek opposition in a series of engagements that on March 17, 1814, culminated with the Battle of Horseshoe Bend.

The following May Jackson was commissioned a major general in the regular army of the United States. He took command of Tennessee, Mississippi, and Louisiana. This move was prophetic on the part of the government. Jackson was sure that the British were planning an eventual move against New Orleans. In order to do that, he knew, they would probably first strike somewhere else on the coast of the Gulf of Mexico. He was right. The British attempted to attack Mobile, Alabama, in September, but Jackson decisively held them off. By November, Jackson had driven the British from their position near Pensacola, Florida. He was now free to take his forces to New Orleans to inspect the defenses at the mouth of the Mississippi River.

Once again Jackson's uncanny ability to think like the enemy paid off. He was in the right place at the right time. In the middle of December the British anchored their fleet of ships at the mouth of the Mississippi and put their troops ashore ten miles south of New Orleans. From there they launched a series of strikes against the city. Jackson countered. The British were no match for the mixture of Louisiana militia, Tennessee and Kentucky riflemen, and a group of pirates from Barataria Bay, a lagoon in southeastern Louisiana. When the British attacked Jackson's troops on January 8, 1815, they were cut down by rifle and cannon fire. Two thousand of their troops were either killed or wounded, as compared with the thirteen American soldiers killed and thirty-nine wounded.

The Battle of New Orleans was the last campaign of the War of 1812. It was actually fought after a peace treaty had been signed in Ghent, Belgium, on December 24, 1814. Many people said that Jackson's victory was won after the war was over, but the treaty actually called for continued hostilities until both the United States and Britain had ratified it. That didn't happen until February 1815.

Finally Americans had a great victory to celebrate. After so many losses, during which the British had burned and sacked Washington, D.C., Americans had begun to question the nation's leadership.

Almost overnight, it seemed, Andrew Jackson had become a true American hero, but the politicians from Virginia were still in charge, and they weren't interested in furthering Jackson's reputation. So Jackson returned to his beloved Hermitage in Nashville to resume his civilian life.

Seminole Indians and runaway slaves from Spanish Florida continued to attack settlements on the Georgia frontier. To stop this, the government recalled Andrew Jackson to active military service in December 1817. He helped force the Indians and the slaves back into Florida.

Around the world the United States was accused of invading sovereign Spanish territory. At first President James Monroe apologized, saying that he had not authorized such an invasion, but then Secretary of State John Quincy Adams persuaded the president to justify the invasion because Spain had failed to keep its citizens from attacking the United States. Because of this, Adams was successful in bringing about the eventual cession of Florida to the United States and favorably redefining the western boundary of the Louisiana Purchase.

On June 1, 1821, Andrew Jackson's military career ended, and he resumed his political career when he was appointed provisional governor of Florida. Even though he resigned this post six months later due to a dispute with President James Monroe, Andrew Jackson had taken the first steps in a journey that would eventually lead him to the White House.

President of the United States

Andrew Jackson became involved in the presidential campaign of 1824 mainly to counter an attempt by local Tennessee politicians to exploit Jackson's fame as a way of guaranteeing the election of one of their cohorts. Jackson was nominated for the presidency by the Tennessee legislature in July 1823. His opponents were Henry Clay of Kentucky, John Quincy Adams of Massachusetts, and William H. Crawford of Georgia (no relation to Jackson). Jackson's opponents, especially Adams, were horrified at the thought of Jackson's becoming president because he was considered a badly educated country bumpkin.

The presidential election of 1824 is often called the "stolen election," because Andrew Jackson won the popular vote decisively, but he did not have enough electoral votes to win the presidency. The election had to be decided by the House of Representatives. Henry Clay and William H. Crawford threw their support to John Quincy Adams on the first ballot, and Adams became the sixth president of the United States. Jackson never forgave them for what they had done.

Jackson and his followers continued to criticize the administration of John Quincy Adams in the years leading up to the presidential election of 1828. Jackson considered himself the candidate of the people. He never missed an opportunity to remind people that he was their choice in the presidential election of 1824, but that the political aristocracy in Washington had ignored that fact. This tactic proved successful. In the 1828 election, Jackson defeated Adams, but in the process, he lost his beloved Rachel. Jackson blamed her death on depression brought about by the malicious gossip surrounding the confusion over their marriage.

Andrew Jackson was the *seventh* president of the United States, but he was the *first* president who didn't come from American political aristocracy, the first to have a vice president resign (John Calhoun), to have married a divorcée, to be nominated at a national convention (in 1832, his second term, in which he defeated Henry Clay), and to use an informal group of advisors, whom he referred to as his "kitchen cabinet."

Andrew Jackson believed in a strong presidency. If he didn't like a piece of legislation, he vetoed it. In fact, he used his veto power more than all of the previous six presidents put together. Jackson also believed in a strong Union—that is, in making sure that the states remained united as the United States. That often brought him into conflict with Southern legislators who thought that if legislation wasn't good for their states, they could just ignore it. Although these problems were eventually solved, similar ones pitting the southern states against the government in Washington would later lead to the American Civil War.

During his presidency Jackson also refused to

recharter the Bank of the United States, because he thought it operated primarily for the benefit of the upper classes at the expense of the working people of the country. The bank ceased to exist when its charter expired in 1836, but Jackson had already weakened it by withdrawing millions of dollars and redistributing the funds among other banks around the country.

The Indian Removal Act was passed in 1830, during Jackson's first administration. This act gave Indians land west of the Mississippi, provided they agreed to leave their tribal homes in the east. Under this law approximately two hundred million acres of traditional tribal land were cleared for white settlement.

During Jackson's presidency two states were admitted to the Union, Arkansas in 1836 and Michigan in 1837.

Andrew Jackson's health was never very good due to his imprisonment during the the American Revolution and his bout with smallpox, and there were times during his presidency when it seemed he would never live to complete his second term.

But he did, and in 1837 he returned to the Hermitage in Nashville.

Jackson still had an interest in national politics, though, and, working behind the scenes, he was successful in securing the presidency for his successor, Martin Van Buren. Jackson also helped to get Texas annexed to the United States.

Toward the end of his life Andrew Jackson's health deteriorated badly, and he died at the Hermitage on June 8, 1845.

Andrew and Rachel had no children of their own, but they did adopt one of Rachel's nephews, whom they named Andrew Jackson Jr. In his will Jackson left the Hermitage to his son, but by 1886 the young Jackson's debts forced him to sell the Hermitage to the state of Tennessee. Today it is open to the public as an historic site, and thousands of people visit it each year.

Read Aladdin Paperbacks' classic biography series,

Childhood of Famous Americans

See your local
bookseller for a full list
of available titles.

**Louisa May Alcott
Young Novelist**
by Beatrice Gormley
0-689-82025-9

**Neil Armstrong
Young Pilot**
by Montrew Dunham
0-689-80995-6

**Roberto Clemente
Young Ball Player**
by Montrew Dunham
0-689-81364-3

**Joe DiMaggio
Young Sports Hero**
by Herb Dunn
0-689-83186-2

**Amelia Earhart
Young Aviator**
by Beatrice Gormley
0-689-83188-9

**Albert Einstein
Young Thinker**
by Marie Hammontree
0-02-041860-4

**Jim Henson
Young Puppeteer**
by Leslie Gourse
0-689-83398-9

**Harry Houdini
Young Magician**
by Kathryn Kilby &
Helen Ross Speicher
0-689-71476-9

**Helen Keller
From Tragedy to
Triumph**
by Katharine E. Wilkie
0-02-041980-5

**Martin Luther King Jr.
Young Man with
a Dream**
by Dharathula H.
Millender
0-02-042010-2

**Abraham Lincoln
The Great
Emancipator**
by Augusta Stevenson
0-02-042030-7

**Thurgood Marshall
Young Justice**
by Montrew Dunham
0-689-82042-9

**John Muir
Young Naturalist**
by Montrew Dunham
0-689-81996-X

**Pocohantas
Young Peacemaker**
by Leslie Gourse
0-689-80808-9

**Ronald Reagan
Young Politician**
by Montrew Dunham
0-689-83006-8

**Jackie Robinson
Young Sports
Trailblazer**
by Herb Dunn
0-689-82453-X

**Babe Ruth
One of Baseball's
Greatest**
by Guernsey Van Riper, Jr.
0-02-042130-3

**George Washington
Young Leader**
by Augusta Stevenson
0-02-042150-8

Aladdin Paperbacks
Simon & Schuster Children's Publishing
www.SimonSaysKids.com